WILDHORSE RANCH BROTHERS

Breaking the Cowboy's Rules

Healing the Quarterback

Stirring up the Sheriff

This is a work of fiction. Names, characters, places and incidents either are the product of imagination or are used fictitiously. Any resemblance to actual persons, living or dead, events or locales, is entirely coincidental.

RELAY PUBLISHING EDITION, APRIL 2017

Copyright © 2017 Relay Publishing Ltd.

All rights reserved. Published in the United Kingdom by Relay Publishing.

No part of this book may be reproduced, published, distributed, displayed, performed, copied or stored for public or private use in any information retrieval system, or transmitted in any form by any mechanical, photographic or electronic process, including electronically or digitally on the Internet or World Wide Web, or over any network, or local area network, without written permission of the author.

Cover Design by LJ Anderson of Mayhem Cover Creations

www.relaypub.com

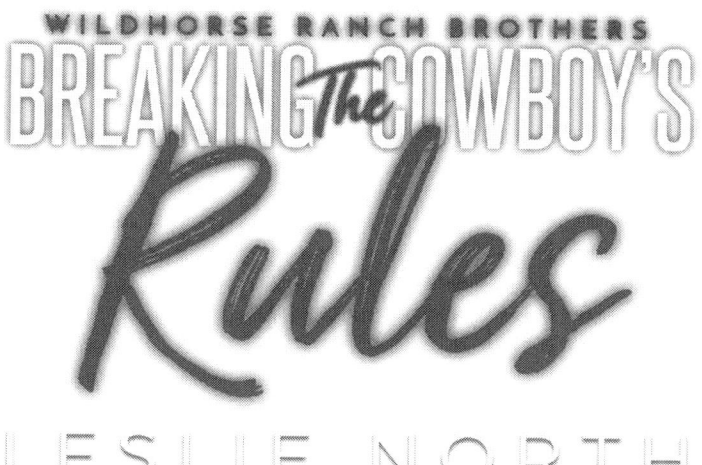

Blurb

Ranch owner, Trevor Wild, loves nothing more than spending his day in the saddle riding in the Texas sun. He's passionate about being the latest generation of Wild man to breed quarter horses on Wildhorse Ranch. But in the aftermath of inheriting a bad business deal the Ranch is in serious financial trouble, and this serious cowboy needs to look outside the box to save his family's pride and joy.

Glamping guru, Sabrina Hearthstone, is the best of the best at what she does, and she could very well be Trevor's saving grace. The blonde beauty arrives at Wildhorse Ranch ready to get the job done. She's all business when it comes to bringing a little luxury to the leather and dirt clad Ranch. But soon she'll realize that to renovate the Ranch for Glamping she may have to renovate its cowboy too.

Sabrina is tempting on a whole lot of levels for Trevor—when he gives into both her touch, and the 1,000 thread count bed sheets, he finds that she soothes his soul. However, Sabrina's world is a difficult thing for the hardened cowboy to accept. Trevor will have to learn to accept Sabrina and her changes to his world, not only to save Wildhorse Ranch, but to save a love he never expected to find.

Thank you for purchasing 'Breaking the Cowboy's Rules' (Wildhorse Ranch Brothers Book One)

Get SIX full-length, highly-rated Leslie North Novellas FREE! Over 548 pages of best-selling romance with a combined 634 FIVE STAR REVIEWS!

Sign-up to her mailing list and get your FREE books: leslienorthbooks.com/sign-up-for-free-books

For all books by Leslie North visit:
Her Website: LeslieNorthBooks.com
Facebook: www.facebook.com/leslienorthbooks

TABLE OF CONTENTS

Chapter 1 1

Chapter 2 18

Chapter 3 26

Chapter 4 42

Chapter 5 59

Chapter 6 73

Chapter 7 90

Chapter 8 103

Chapter 9 112

Chapter 10 124

Chapter 11 136

Epilogue 142

Sneak Peek 150

Chapter 1
Trevor

"That her?" Trevor Wild asked his brother. The question rose from his lips like vapor, his warm breath chilled by contact with the early morning air.

He already knew the answer to his question, but he wanted to make sure he wasn't hallucinating the pretty blonde woman standing in front of the old bunkhouse with her arms crossed. She appeared to be in deep contemplation of the woodpile he had been gathering there all season, and the intensity of her concentration made her blind to everything else—including the two men watching her from behind the fence across the property.

"That's her," his brother confirmed. Trent hitched the front of his Wranglers up and blew casually on a steaming mug of coffee he had lifted out of the ranch kitchen. Trevor, sleep-deprived from his long drive home from the conference, felt a surge of jealousy at his twin's morning alertness. "Sabrina Hearthstone, Wildhorse Ranch's very own Glamping Adventure Coordinator. I'd say it has a certain ring to it, but I'm not sure half of those words were meant to exist in the English language."

Trevor cringed in private agreement, the shadow of his hat brim concealing his reaction to the distasteful word. "Glamping," a portmanteau of *glamorous camping,* was not a concept he had ever imagined, let alone expected to put into place at Wildhorse. At thirty-two, he was sure life had more unpleasant revelations in store for him, but whether Sabrina Hearthstone might be the next unfortunate event in a glamping-related string of surprises remained to be seen.

"Looks like you're going to have your hands full with this one," Trent remarked as the distant female figure pulled her hair back into a ponytail and dropped to a squat. He said it in the tone of a horseman surveying a particularly unruly filly. Trevor wondered what his brother had gone through already with this woman; still, there was no mistaking the slight tone of admiration in Trent's voice.

"Looks like she's got her hands plenty full already," Trevor mentioned. He squinted across the lawn at Sabrina, who appeared to be dismantling and hauling much of the woodpile up onto the porch. "What the hell is she doing?"

That scrap was probably lousy with splinters—not to mention pill bugs and termites—yet she didn't shrink from grappling with it barehanded. She might as well have been holding the front door wide open and inviting the pests to brunch in the goddamn bunkhouse living room.

"No idea," Trent replied, before amending. "I thought she said something about wanting the scraps for planters or a coffee table or something. You know, like a project."

Trevor sighed and cuffed his brother on the shoulder. "Thanks for keeping an eye on the place while I was away." He tipped his hat in advance of another momentary farewell. "You want to stick around for a bit? Give me the rundown of what's been going on?"

"Sure. Not like I have a job or anything."

The grim line of Trevor's mouth flexed a little. "I'll catch up with you in a few, Sheriff."

"You know I'll be here. And get some coffee!" Trent hollered the suggestion after him. "Something tells me you're going to need it!"

Something tells me you're right. What he wouldn't do for a cup as black as Sabrina Hearthstone was fair. Despite feeling dead on his feet, Trevor loped the length of the yard to reach the new adventure coordinator. She glanced up when she heard his bootsteps; she opened her mouth to start talking almost before he was within earshot.

"Oh! I'm so glad you're here, Trent. Do you mind helping me with this monster?" Sabrina wiped her forehead and indicated the log giving her trouble. Trevor knew it all too well. Not only had he struggled for more hours than he would readily admit to unearth it and drag it this far, but his unwillingness to move it again was the entire reason the wood scrap on his property had started accumulating here in the first place.

Trevor doubted a pair of freckled, toothpick-thin arms would provide the help he needed to haul it, but he had never turned down a woman in distress before. "Sure." He pulled on his work gloves and stooped to wrestle the other end of the log into his arms. "But I'm not Trent."

"Huh?" Sabrina glanced up to take him in again, and dropped the side of the log she was holding. Trevor grimaced and set his end down, also. The way his mouth tended to frown naturally—and only deepen when he was annoyed or working—distinguished him from his more approachable twin brother.

"No...I mean, *wow*. You really aren't, are you?" Now that Sabrina had halted operations, Trevor straightened to regard her in turn. The way she looked him over, with eyes as wide and summer-blue as the Texas sky, made him acutely aware of just how closely they stood.

"No. I really am not," he agreed. He wondered how much Trent let her get away with while he was gone. Sabrina Hearthstone had a face as pretty as an angel's—pair that with her ridiculously tight, stone-washed designer jeans, and he doubted his brother had been willing to deny her much. She was the living, breathing lyric of a country song standing before him—the worshipped, vaunted *city girl*—and for the first time, Trevor contemplated how much trouble he might be in having her on his property.

At least they had managed to agree on one important detail so far: he wasn't his brother Trent. While the Sheriff of Lockhart Bend might be willing to let certain behaviors slide, Trevor expected a rigid adherence to his rules. If she already found him more serious, more commanding, than his twin brother, then it might make his job a hell of a lot easier.

"So, you must be Trevor," Sabrina deduced. "The owner. Unless you're triplets I wasn't aware of," she appeared to mutter to herself. She extended a slender hand to him, and Trevor removed one of his gloves before taking it in his own. He wondered what his callouses must feel like rubbing against her soft skin. She didn't draw back immediately, which he also found curious. They held the handshake a few seconds longer than strictly necessary before Sabrina withdrew and flushed a little.

"Sorry I mistook you for your brother," she apologized. "I guess I didn't realize you'd be back today."

"I keep to a schedule," Trevor stated. "Which is something you're throwing off already, Miss Hearthstone." He nodded toward the scraps she had accumulated on the porch. "I'm tossing that wood out in the quarterly clear-out." She stared at him blankly. "That's tomorrow. You want to keep any of it for arts and crafts, I expect you to go through it all today."

"Excuse me, Mr. Wild, but this isn't for *arts and crafts,*" Sabrina protested. She gestured toward her woodpile selections. "This is upcycling! I'm going to make good use of this stuff. If we want to attract customers and garner favorable reviews, then we're going to need to liven up the living spaces with a few rustic decorations."

Upcycling. Great. Another made-up word. Trevor hooked his thumbs in his belt and didn't budge an inch, predicting his silence would be enough to settle the matter. Generally speaking, it was. Today, however, his natural powers of intimidation appeared to be diminished after the long drive. Sabrina had her hands on her hips, her dark pink lips pursed in challenge. For the life of him he couldn't decide if her expression was meant to convey a fight or invite a kiss.

"And it's going to take me longer than a day to figure out what I can and can't use here," she clarified.

"You signed a contract," he said. "And part of that contract clearly states you agree to adhere to the ranch's schedule." *And my rules,* he was going to add, before Sabrina interrupted him unexpectedly.

"How about time for coffee?" she said. She turned away from him to start up the front steps to the porch, before throwing offhand over her shoulder: "I assume there's room in the ranch's schedule for that?"

The offer sounded like a tactical maneuver rather than a true invitation, but he followed her up the steps to the bunkhouse despite his suspicion. He couldn't help noticing the sequins studded around the back pockets of her jeans. The detail—*and only that detail*—drew his attention to Sabrina's pert hindquarters. She sure could fill a pair of impractical pants. The denim might as well have been painted onto those shapely, athletic legs of hers. He doubted she could fully bend over in them but would have been willing to be proved wrong.

"You were at a conference, right? How did it go?" Sabrina smiled perkily as she took the bunkhouse pot off the burner and poured them each a mug of coffee. Trevor hovered in the doorway, studying her change in expression and still wondering if he was being taken for a ride. He would have thought then that she certainly had the cheerful demeanor to be successful in her chosen profession...*if* he didn't still have doubts that her chosen profession actually existed.

"It went fine." The impromptu conference had given him a lot to chew on, and he felt cautiously optimistic about the future of Wildhorse's breeding program for the first time since he had taken a chance and hired an adventure coordinator. If he was being honest with himself, he didn't like the fact that he had to call on Trent to help Sabrina move in. Trevor was the ranch owner, and he would have rather seen to the matter himself—but his meeting with the other breeders in the area couldn't be put on hold.

He accepted the mug of coffee Sabrina handed him and settled back against the porch railing. The blonde leaned against the outside of the bunkhouse, crossing her legs and folding her arms, pursing her kissable lips and blowing steam off her own mug.

"I got in touch with your company originally because the ranch needs another source of income," he began.

"Obviously." She flexed a grin to let him know she was on the same page.

"But I'm not giving up the quarter horse breeding program. It's what we've done here for three generations, since my grandad's day. It's the heart and soul of this ranch, and it's what Wildhorse is known for." Trevor scowled, hoping to stamp his next point home. "So, I don't want our programs intersecting, Miss Hearthstone. You see to coordinating the campers and keep them out of my hair, and I go about my business as usual, including paying your company's fee."

"Fine, Mr. Wild. Just so long as you understand what I most certainly *won't* be doing is keeping our campers out of the stables," Sabrina fired back. "You can't expect anyone to have even a half-baked glamping experience—nor can you expect them to spread positive word-of-mouth and leave us glowing reviews—if our customers aren't even allowed to *experience* the horses. You tell me what barns to stay out of, and I will—but judging by the tour Trent gave me, there's plenty of stable space for all of us. Besides," Sabrina continued as she smiled once more, "contrary to what you may think, I've been around horses before. I happen to know that most ranch animals enjoy the extra attention and go on to live happy, more fulfilled lives as a result. You wouldn't deny your horses that, would you?"

Trevor didn't like that she was pushing for such a huge compromise already, but now seemed like the perfect time to segue into what he really wanted to talk about: rules. He withdrew a folded set of documents from the inner pocket of his jacket and passed them to her.

"Then you stick to the schedule I've laid out for you," he said. He allowed himself a moment to privately relish the look of horror that crossed her face. He had guessed from the start that she was the type of woman to flout the rules, but he intended to put an end to that behavior before it had even begun. He sipped his coffee and watched as Sabrina riffled through the multi-page document.

"This is…why are there *checklists?"* she asked incredulously. She rattled the pages at him. "Do you actually expect me to fill these out and turn them back in to you?"

"I expect you to read them over and know how things work around here," Trevor replied. "I run a tight ship, Miss Hearthstone. A ranch this size doesn't operate without a strict schedule and systematic chores that go along with it. Everyone pulls their weight on a ranch, and Wildhorse's adventure coordinator is no exception."

"As you've so bluntly stated, you're funding my paycheck," Sabrina muttered. "But I guess I was hoping you would consider me more of a collaborator than an employee."

Trevor paused to absorb this. All the while, Sabrina gazed back at him with the first somber expression he had seen out of the energetic woman. He had intended to control that fire he saw, not snuff it.

But what she said deserved some reflection. While his brother had a vested interest in Wildhorse, Trent led his own life in town. Most of the responsibility fell on Trevor's shoulders, and he was more than happy to bear the brunt of it.

But Sabrina was offering to shoulder some of that burden also. Not only that, she wanted to be his active collaborator—she only fought his insistence that they operate separately because she thought the ranch would benefit from a partnership.

At least, that's what he was reading into her imploring look. She may have been a city girl, an outsider thrust into the middle of his carefully-ordered world, but that didn't preclude a certain amount of business savvy. If anything, he should probably expect it from her.

"All right. Collaborators," Trevor agreed. He sealed their agreement by raising his coffee, all the while eyeing her from beneath the wide brim of his hat. "Do me a favor and look those over anyway. It'll be important for you to know what hours I'll be in the stables. We can come together again once you've familiarized yourself with the schedule to work out times for camper activities."

"Fine." Sabrina smiled, and proceeded to roll his documents up. She used the resulting tube to point toward the woodpile. "But I'm going to need extra time with your wood. I mean...!" She flushed as Trevor looked on in amusement. He might not have even noticed the slip if it weren't for the immediate look of mortification that passed across her face. "What I *meant* to say was, I don't think I'll be able to adhere to that part of the schedule," she stated. "You can't rush art, Mr. Wild."

"Art," he echoed her in a deadpan voice.

"I'll take personal responsibility and get rid of any scrap when I'm done," she insisted. "You can depend on me to keep my word. And besides..." Sabrina's smile brightened like a sunbeam as she gave him the thumbs-up. "You're not going to regret what I have in store."

Trevor exhaled through his nose in frustration. "I think I already do," he muttered. He drained the rest of his coffee and set his mug down on the railing. "All right, Miss Hearthstone," he said. "We'll catch up with one another tomorrow. Come find me in the stables once you've familiarized yourself with the schedule."

"Should I call beforehand to make an appointment?" Sabrina asked as he stepped down off the porch.

Trevor said nothing in response; just tipped his hat brim in farewell, deepening the shadows across his face and hiding the way his mouth twitched slightly upward despite his best efforts.

*   *   *

"Well, I happen to think Sabrina's a great addition," Trent said. "Spunky. Beautiful."

The sun had risen to take its noontime place in the sky, and the two brothers had retreated inside the easternmost stable block to escape its rays for a bit. Trevor had shed his coat hours ago and now had his sleeves rolled up. He plunged elbow-deep into one of the metal water troughs he had brought in from the pasture, scrubbing off the algae and crud that had accumulated over the last three months.

"Two out of three isn't bad," Trevor said cryptically from inside the tub.

He heard Trent chuckle. His brother leaned in the aisle, chewing a piece of straw and doing little else to be constructive. Apparently, now that Trevor had returned to take the lead on things, Trent thought he had earned himself a break from chores. "Leave it to you to make a checklist for a woman," his brother replied eventually. "No wonder you're still single."

"You're one to talk." Trevor used the back of his wrist to wipe the sweat from his forehead as he rose. "How long you been without a woman now?"

"You're right." Trent grimaced. "Must have less to do with organization and more to do with our damn looks. I forget sometimes we share the same genes."

Trent may have been Trevor's identical twin, but their disparate personalities had manifested themselves physically long ago. It sometimes felt to Trevor like he was looking in a funhouse mirror, where every feature was the same yet somehow inverted, rather than directly at his twin. Trevor found the time to shave less often than his brother did, and his skin was dark in comparison to Trent's town-tan. The heels of their work boots still made them equally tall, and the physical activity required by their professions made them equally broad, but Trent's face was a lot pleasanter to look at, or so Trevor thought. His brother gave up a smile or laugh far more readily, and he put people at ease with no effort at all; he had laugh lines to Trevor's frown lines.

Trent's identical dark eyes sparked with humor all of a sudden. Trevor had the distinct feeling he was about to find out he was the punchline to some secret joke his brother kept, but was surprised by Trent's next comment. "Might share the same taste in women, too," Trent hinted.

An image of Sabrina came unbidden into Trevor's head. For a city girl, she was just about everything he had been expecting her to be, down to her impractical designer jeans, and yet...their first encounter had left him feeling strangely winded. He couldn't be certain it wasn't all the breath he had expended on arguing with her. She had an animation and energy to her that the profile picture on her company's website simply hadn't been able to convey.

So yes, at the end of the day, Sabrina Hearthstone had surprised Trevor. He wouldn't deny that he found her attractive, and something told him her eager personality was just as magnetic to anyone who happened to enter her orbit. Personally, he didn't know what to make of it.

Still, if Trent insisted on continually throwing the adventure coordinator at him as a distraction, he supposed he would have to set his brother straight. "I can't speak to taste," he said finally, "but what we don't share is the same opinion about things. This whole 'glamping' thing is just a temporary means to an end," he reminded his brother. "The ranch is still going to operate like it always has. Once we're out of the red, I'll cut the adventure program and send Miss Hearthstone and her glue gun on their way to bedazzle someplace else."

"Does Sabrina know that?" Trent asked.

"Miss Hearthstone and I have reached an understanding," Trevor said curtly. "She stays out of my side of the business, and I stay out of hers. We come together to discuss any overlap. At the end of the day, nothing happens on this ranch without my stamp of approval. Same as it's been since Grandpa passed."

"You know, it might not be a bad idea to consider changing with the times," Trent reminded him. They'd had this conversation more than once since the untimely death of their grandfather, and Trevor never warmed to it. Change, and one as significant as what his brother hinted at, wouldn't so easily fit into the schedule, even if he wanted it to begin with.

"Grandpa James was a good man," Trent continued. "He didn't mean to leave you in a hole…"

"I'm sure he didn't mean to leave at all," Trevor grunted.

"But he wouldn't want you to *stay* in that hole on his account either, Trev. Hell, you're a horseman. You know better than I do that the most recent stock he purchased isn't paying for itself. And without them, you don't have the money to make that balloon payment he still owes," Trent concluded. "Wildhorse doesn't have to *just* breed quarter horses. Why don't you admit this glamping program is a good idea? It might just be the thing that saves your sorry ass and keeps the ranch operating for another season."

"I'll find a way out of this on my own." Trevor turned away to work a kink out in the hose. "Always have before. More importantly, the *ranch* will find its way out. So, you don't need to worry yourself with trying to retroactively contribute to the family legacy. Grandpa didn't expect you to care about this sort of thing before, and I certainly don't expect you to start caring now."

"And when this sort of thing happens again?" his brother demanded angrily. Trevor could see that he had hit a sore point, and it wasn't exactly unintentional. A part of him felt guilty for continually stonewalling his brother, but another part knew it was only a matter of time before Trent threw up his hands and walked away. "You could have the most successful breeding program in the world, and you're still going to run into this sort of trouble again down the line! It's inevitable!" Trent exclaimed. "You need a back-up plan for the long haul, brother. You *need* a gal like Sabrina bringing fresh ideas to the table. Lord knows you don't listen to me—maybe you'll be more likely to listen to reason when it comes from a beauty in blue jeans."

"Sabrina doesn't belong here!" Trevor snapped. The stable block descended into silence. When Trent didn't respond immediately, Trevor glanced up from his work to see if his rise in temper had caused his brother to retreat. Trent was leaning on the other side of the aisle, same as before, only this time he appeared to be keenly studying him.

"Then send her back and choose another coordinator," his brother stated finally. "Hell, choose another program. One that better suits your narrow idea of what you think this place is. One that you're *comfortable* dealing with."

"I'll deal with Miss Hearthstone just fine," Trevor responded as he kneeled to scrub once more. "So long as she follows my rules."

CHAPTER 2
SABRINA

"And I was *thinking* we could pair each guest up with one of the ranch hands for a day," Sabrina continued excitedly, her pink ostrich feather pen wagging behind her clipboard as she jotted down elaborations on her idea. "Maybe Tuesday? Because according to the schedule you left me, Mr. Wild, there appears to be plenty of time in the later hours of the morning on the ranch's slow day—"

"No such thing as a slow day," Trevor interrupted her.

The wagging pen paused, and Sabrina closed her throat quickly over a sigh of exasperation. They had been going at it all morning like this. She was currently perched on a stall partition, trying—and failing—to get Trevor's undivided attention. Wildhorse's taciturn owner was currently shoveling out the stall across the aisle from her own, the bunched muscles of his back offering her few clear signals about how well she was communicating her ideas.

She privately suspected he had chosen the location of their first meeting for a reason, and one that had only partially to do with the chores he insisted couldn't wait. Well, if Trevor had thought that all the dust in the air and the pervading smell of horse manure would be enough to drive her away, he had thought dead wrong.

Sabrina's grandparents, Forest and Harriet Hearthstone, had been the proud owners of their own ranch until their health had forced them to sell it, and Sabrina was no stranger to the filthier aspects of horse upkeep. In fact, there was a particular, even overpowering, nostalgia factor to this life that she continued to seek out. Why else would she take so readily to a job that pushed her out of the city? Why else would she be so damn *good* at it?

If only Trevor would accept that she was the sort of professional he needed! Sabrina's eyes narrowed in a secret glare at the rancher's back, taking in the triangular sweat stain that darkened his shirt between his powerful shoulders. She wasn't afraid to sweat, and she certainly wasn't afraid of hard work—it just so happened that *hard work* came in many forms.

She caught sight of the frilly pen out of the corner of her eye. Was it the pen that made him doubt her? It had been a gag gift from a friend. She could get another pen.

"Right. No such thing as a slow day," she echoed. "But you have to allow your workers a break, right? So why not give them a little additional time out of their day to show our guests around?"

"Because I don't have any hands to spare for that sort of thing, end of story," Trevor stated. He heaved a shovelful of manure over his shoulder without looking, forcing Sabrina to dodge to the side to avoid some of the dirt that overshot the wheelbarrow. "I already let most of the seasonal workers go to cut costs. The ones who stayed understand that they already have their work cut out for them this year."

"Well, that's the beauty of my plan, Mr. Wild," Sabrina replied patiently. "You won't need to 'spare' anyone. And as for cutting costs, by the time I'm done spinning things, our guests will be happy to follow the ranch hands around and help them with their chores. They are effectively paying *you* for the chance to experience all that Wildhorse has to offer—and that includes discovering what it really takes to keep a ranch like this running."

Trevor paused in his shoveling and finally turned to look at her. Sabrina couldn't decide whether he was incredulous of her brilliant idea or dubious that she wasn't completely out of her mind. What she did know in that moment was that sweat and dirt only made the rancher appear more irresistibly rugged.

He's the real deal, Sabrina thought. As much as she hated to admit it, she was a little in awe of Trevor Wild. She had been operating under the misconception that real cowboys had died out long ago, but one stood before her, a flesh-and-blood update to that vintage romantic trope.

The adventure coordinator in her couldn't help but think the stoic ranch owner might unwittingly prove to be one of

Wildhorse's main attractions. Market research told her that their clientele would be made up of almost exclusively city women and upper middle-class families. She knew from past experience that families had a way of occupying themselves, but women....

Deep down, Sabrina felt certain that what every woman wished for was fantasy. Enchantment. A little bit of grit mixed in with their decadence, an introduction to a simple yet lavish reality they had always suspected existed far removed from their own. They wanted an escape from the rat race and responsibility—they wanted the chance to return to the outgrown idealism of their girlhood, where wonderful beasts and handsome princes and *all* of life's hardships could be tamed with a brave outlook and a gentle touch.

And she, Sabrina Hearthstone, could fulfill that longing for them—finally make those seemingly far-fetched fantasies a reality. It was the best job in the world, as far as she was concerned.

So, whether he liked it or not, she was going to have to promote Trevor Wild a bit, even if she had to do it behind his back. Some candid shots of the rancher posted to Wildhorse's social media accounts ought to get a few hearts racing. The fact that she was using her own heartbeat as a gauge just went to show how *personally* she took her work.

Trevor removed his hat and perched it on the post beside him, revealing a head of close-cropped dark hair. He then reached down, grabbing a fistful of T-shirt, and Sabrina...well, she nearly fell over backwards into the stall in surprise. The thought of him actually *removing* his shirt hit her like a sucker punch in the stomach, and she quickly raised her clipboard to block her own view and pretended to scribble quickly.

Wait...why was she acting this way? She was a grown woman! It wasn't like she had never seen a partially-naked man before, even if it had been a while.

Sabrina lowered her clipboard and studied the rancher. As it turned out, Trevor was only using the hem of his T-shirt to mop some of the sweat and grime off his face. Her eyes tracked lower, taking in his smooth chest and the way his abdominal muscles clenched beneath a sheen of perspiration. For someone who insisted on wearing a belt, his pants sure rode low around his hips....

Trevor's strength, when on unconscious display this way, seemed completely natural and effortless. She doubted if he had a gym membership or if such a conceit had ever even crossed his mind—endless days full of hard work toned his body to perfection. He probably didn't even *know* how good he looked.

In the next instant, he let go of his T-shirt and turned back to the wheelbarrow. The spell broke, and Sabrina blinked. The moment had taken her by complete surprise, and she was unsure what it might bode for the future. She had never had to battle her admiration for a client before. She had never had to battle *any* client before as fiercely as Trevor was forcing her to.

"You want to watch it with those," he mentioned offhandedly.

Sabrina blinked again. "Huh?"

Trevor gestured toward her earrings, a pair of sterling silver hoops designed as horseshoes, which Sabrina had designed herself and was extremely proud of. "Your jewelry. You want to watch it, especially if you insist on sitting on the stall door like that. All it takes is one tug from a curious horse come in from the pasture to put you over the side."

It's not the horses I'm worried about, she thought mutinously. She fingered her earlobe and scowled. She may or may not have been expecting a compliment with her choice, but she simply could not win his approval.

"I don't want to know your opinion on my fashion choices, Mr. Wild."

"Really?" he asked as he turned back to his work. "Because I have a lot of them, and they aren't just opinions. I would make you a list of everything you've worn already that isn't ranch-appropriate or poses a safety hazard, but I'm not certain you'd have anything left to wear."

"I'm sure you would make a list!" Sabrina fired back. "But I'm a professional woman. I know how to dress myself, and what I choose to wear isn't up for discussion. What I would *really* like to hear from you is some constructive feedback on the ideas I've been pitching to you all morning!" She rapped the clipboard with her pen to emphasize this. "And every single brainstorm I've come up with you've shot down like a...like a can of beans on a fence post!"

Trevor groaned at the simile. "I'm not trying to shoot your ideas down, Miss Hearthstone." Sabrina scoffed at this, and Trevor shot her a look that conveyed his wearying patience. "Forgive me if I don't think our guests are going to want to muck out stalls after their bubble baths," he muttered as he levered the wheelbarrow up and moved it to the next stall.

The lightbulb went on suddenly in Sabrina's head. Her pen paused its tapping, and she looked up at Trevor. "Mr. Wild, you may not look it, but you're a genius," she said.

"You city folks sure love to pair an insult with a compliment," he said. Still, he paused again in his work to lean against the stall and consider her, his dark eyes thoughtful. "What brilliant thing did I say, and why do I have a feeling I'm going to regret ever mentioning it?"

Sabrina dropped her clipboard onto the footstool beneath her and hopped down after it. "I think this idea is best expressed through a demonstration," she said. "And since you were the inspiration for it, Mr. Wild, I think it's only fitting that *you're* the one who helps me."

Chapter 3
TREVOR

"I still can't believe I let you talk me into this," Trevor muttered a half hour later.

They stood together in the aisle with the barn door flung open. Peggy, one of the older, gentler mares in the Wildhorse herd, stood placidly between them, shifting her weight every few minutes and aiming a switch of her tail at the occasional fly.

Sabrina ducked beneath the lead rope and grinned, taking one hand from Peggy's neck to give him a thumbs-up. She had taken her ridiculous earrings out, at least, and pulled her hair into a silky blonde ponytail. Peggy took it upon herself to investigate whether the woman's unfamiliar hairstyle was as delectable as it looked. Sabrina laughed and pushed her away again.

"Relax," she assured him. "I can already tell this girl is a real sweetheart. This is going to be a piece of cake!"

"Have you ever bathed a horse before?" Trevor asked, raising an eyebrow in disbelief. Sabrina's instincts around horses and the easy way she carried herself around Peggy had surprised him more than he cared to admit. She had more experience than he had anticipated, and a dim curiosity kindled in him every time he looked at her. What was her history? Her story? Was there more to the adventure coordinator than her doomed attempts to glamorize a lifestyle he had assumed she knew nothing about?

Clearly, she did know a thing or two, and Trevor couldn't help but feel the need to find out more.

"How hard can it be?" Sabrina rolled her sleeves up and dropped to a squat beside the big metal wash bucket. "I mean, *really*. It can't be that different from bathing a dog. Trust me, our campers are going to love this." She popped open the bottle of scented bath soap she had retrieved from her bunkhouse and let a little more spill into the swirling tub. "Not only do they get the chance to bond with individual horses and actively participate in spreading the luxury around, but *you* get clean, shiny ponies at the end of the day. Everyone's happy and fulfilled. It's a win-win!"

In the face of such blinding optimism, Trevor didn't know how to fight back—what's more, the sight of Sabrina's slender neck unobstructed by hair was proving unusually distracting for him. The suds started bubbling up in the tub, and a rich coconut aroma rose into the air. He imagined this must be what a spa in the Caribbean smelled like. He shot a paranoid look over his shoulder, but there was no one in the immediate vicinity to witness his folly. He was certain that if his brother stumbled upon them now, he would never hear the end of it.

"There!" Sabrina said brightly. She rose and twisted the spigot off. Peggy's ears perked forward, and the horse pawed the ground expectantly. Sabrina laughed. "See? She likes it already! At least *someone* thinks my ideas are good."

"I don't think your ideas are bad," Trevor muttered. Sabrina glanced up in surprise from caressing Peggy's nose, and he felt a little hot under the collar all of a sudden. He hadn't expected her to take his remark to heart. Maybe he had made worse of an impression on her than he had guessed, if she thought his outreach so surprising now. "Not all of them, anyway," he amended.

He moved a little closer, laying his broad, bare hand on the mare's opposite cheek. Peggy snorted and nodded, evidently pleased with all the attention she was receiving. "I appreciate that you're trying to marry every harebrained idea you have with what's best for the horses, Miss Hearthstone."

"Please," she interrupted. "If your brother can call me 'Sabrina,' then so can you." She grinned. "Besides, it will look good in front of the guests if we already have a rapport established. It will make it seem like we're on the same page...even if that isn't always the case."

Trevor crooked a smile and shifted his weight. "Well then, Sabrina, you're going to want to take that top off." He indicated her pink checkered shirt with a sweep of his hand and was amused when he saw her cheeks darken to a similar hue. The subtext of his unexpected comment wasn't lost on him. "Peggy's a doll, but she isn't a Barbie doll," he continued. "You think the idea of a bath gets her excited now, just wait till the hose comes out again and the suds start flying. Things'll go a lot easier the less heavy clothes you're wearing."

"Good point," Sabrina said thoughtfully. "Now that you mention it...."

Trevor watched as Sabrina moved back to strip her outer layer off her shoulders, revealing that the smooth, bare skin of her collar bone was as freckle-dusted as her nose. Trevor swallowed and kept his expression carefully neutral even as she turned from him to toss her shirt over the stable door. Something as simple as an unexpected smattering of freckles shouldn't come as a revelation to him, but he couldn't deny the sight's appeal—especially on a woman already as effortlessly lovely as Sabrina. She obviously wasn't afraid to let the summer sun come out and kiss that porcelain complexion of hers.

"There." She fluffed her ponytail to fullness and turned back to Trevor. "Is this better?" She stood before him now clad in a white T-shirt and jeans, which he supposed was the best he could ask for.

"Gonna guess I can't convince you to get out of those," he said, gesturing with the end of Peggy's lead rope to Sabrina's skinny jeans.

Sabrina grinned. "Not unless you want to turn this into a bikini horse wash."

"I'll just bet you have a bikini packed away in your suitcase somewhere," he muttered.

"That's for me to know and you to never find out," the adventure coordinator teased him. "Well, unless you have a Jacuzzi hidden around here somewhere that I don't know about, Mr. Wild."

"Not a lot of Jacuzzis out in this part of the country. I think this is as close as you're going to get," he replied. "All right. First things first." He picked up a curry comb and passed it across Peggy's back to Sabrina. "Go down her side and work the dirt and dust out of her coat. Then take the body brush, there," he pointed toward the next brush arrayed on the bench, "and go over her a second time to make sure she's clean. You start in on bathing her first, and you're going to wind up with a mud-caked horse that smells like a damn cupcake."

"You hear that? He likes that smell," Sabrina confided in Peggy. "Maybe I shouldn't tell him it's my body wash we're using."

The thought had already crossed his mind, of course, and he had just as quickly banished the mental image that went along with it. He didn't need to know that Sabrina Hearthstone smelled as good as she looked. But he also hadn't told her where to find the ranch's supply of soap they normally used on the horses.

They worked down the length of the mare in relative silence, communicating their progress through little puffs of dust that erupted into the air beneath their brushes. "Good," Trevor said after a while. "See how relaxed she is? If you want to pursue this crazy idea of yours, you're going to want to encourage trust between the horse and camper. We brush them down like this twice a day, so it's something they're used to already. It makes them feel good and signals to them that they're in capable hands. They'll be more likely to trust you with whatever potions you want to throw at them after this."

"May I give her a sugar cube?" Sabrina inquired. Trevor nodded, and watched as she plucked two from the box on the bench: one for Peggy, and one for herself. The adventure coordinator held his eyes as she popped the second one mischievously into her mouth. Trevor experienced an immediate, impulsive desire to reclaim it—using his own mouth, preferably.

He shook his head to clear it quickly. Sabrina watched him, tonguing the cube around behind her perfect teeth, and crunched down with a grin. She was teasing him, but the angelic quality of her smile told him she had no idea what part of him *specifically* she was teasing. Maybe their first meeting had been effective after all in establishing a cold front—even if he felt anything but cold toward Sabrina right now.

"Comb out her mane next," he said gruffly. "Use the curry comb if you want. I'll go around back and get her tail. After that, we'll start in with the water."

"Yes, sir," Sabrina said as she moved to the front of the mare. Once they'd groomed Peggy from tip to tail, they reconvened by the suds bucket. Trevor passed Sabrina a sponge and a jelly scrubber.

"I'll let you lead on this," he said.

To his surprise, Sabrina glanced at him uncertainly. "I…well, you're doing a great job directing me so far," she admitted. "If you give me instructions, I'll feel more confident relaying them to our guests—knowing they came from you."

Trevor said nothing in response. As Sabrina rose from wetting her sponge, he quietly assumed a position behind her to keep up his instructions. The crown of her head barely came up to his chin. When she turned to look back at him, she seemed taken by surprise by their height difference. Her eyebrows rose as she glanced up the length of his chest. She gave her head a little shake and turned back to the horse.

"Start here?" she suggested. She began to soap Peggy's neck in slow rotations. The horse whickered.

"Right," Trevor agreed. "Start back up at the head. She trusts you by now, but the sponge and soap and water are less expected than the brush was. Give her time to adjust and see what you're doing."

"How about you?" Sabrina inquired offhand. "Have you had enough time to…adjust…to me yet? Or do you still not trust me?"

"I trust you." He responded automatically, and he wondered if he should have actually thought about his answer first. "Your heart's in the right place."

"But you don't think my ideas are sound," she argued. "You might think my heart is in the right place, Mr. Wild, but you also think my head's in the clouds. To you I'm all blonde hair, fun earrings and coconut-scented oils and bubbles, but I'm as hard a worker as you are. I just have different goals. I want to help the people who devote their lives to unglamorous chores, like you do, feel special. I want to help them relax."

"Relax," Trevor echoed her. His hands found her shoulders and he paused her work. "Peggy can tell that you're tense."

"Am I?" Sabrina's voice wavered a little. "I hadn't noticed."

Trevor let his hands slide down the slope of her shoulders. He felt it when some of Sabrina's tension eased out of her posture, and she relaxed back into him slightly. "Better," he coaxed her. "Remember that horses can sense the emotions you project. That's probably something you want to tell our guests."

"Our guests?" she repeated as she resumed washing Peggy. "Does that mean you'll be involved after all?"

"It's my ranch," Trevor reminded her. "I'm involved in everything that goes on here whether I like it or not."

"What about Trent? Doesn't he help you?"

"Trent has his own life to lead. He has a share in Wildhorse, but that's about it. I try not to ask more of him," Trevor said. "He volunteered to help you settle in while I was away."

"He's a good man." Sabrina hesitated. "You both are. Your grandfather…he's the one who raised you?"

"After dad died in a riding accident. I was seventeen."

Sabrina stopped washing at this revelation. Trevor reached along the length of her arm and wove his fingers with hers to encourage her to keep going with the sponge.

"And your mother…"

"Before that. She died in childbirth." Trevor kept the hand on hers steady. "My father remarried. After his death, my stepmother, Pam, moved back to Austin with my half-brother, Charlie. She was a hard-working woman, but never cut out for this life—her heart wasn't in it."

Trevor fell silent. He watched over Sabrina's shoulder as their joined hands continued to work the lather into Peggy's coat in slow, relaxing circles.

"They both have their lives to lead. I was ready to begin my life as an adult and take on the work I inherited here. We still keep in touch and do holidays together."

"Wow, that's…" Sabrina tucked a loose strand of hair behind one ear with her free hand as she absorbed his story. Finally, she gave a little laugh. "I can't believe *you* of all people just opened up to me like that. I guess this coconut bubble bath wasn't exaggerating the magical properties it boasts about on the bottle."

"I have no problem talking about myself or my life," Trevor stated. "I'm just not given to talking about them often."

"Or talking at all," Sabrina supplied, with a hint of irony in her tone.

"I've been plenty talkative with you," he pointed out. "Just didn't think you were especially open to hearing what I had to say."

"I'm not open to what *you* have to say?" Sabrina turned halfway around in his arms in astonishment, and Trevor realized

for the first time the real implications of how close they were standing to one another. Guiding the woman from behind had felt like harmless flirtation before, but having her lips this close to his own was a definite threat to the professionalism they had fought to establish.

"You're right," he amended quickly. "You've been surprisingly open to compromise. I misjudged you."

"Thank you." Sabrina spun back around to face Peggy, and the moment passed without her ever having noticed it begin. Trevor stifled a sigh of relief and pressed his chest close to her back once more as he resumed guiding her.

"You have nice hands," he mentioned as he enclosed her hand in his and directed the next sweep of the sponge. "They're soft. If you're going to follow me around and get in the thick of things, you're going to want a pair of work gloves to protect them."

"I'm honestly trying to decide if I should feel complimented," she said. "Seems to me a man like you wouldn't find much to admire in a city girl's hands. I wish I had more callouses."

"You'll get there." He didn't pull away from touching her until they had finished soaping Peggy's side together. Sabrina bent to squeeze the sponge out, and shot an amused look over her shoulder.

"Does that mean you're going to let me stick around for a little while, Mr. Wild?" she asked him.

"Trevor," he corrected automatically. "You wanted to establish a rapport, remember? It sounds unequal when I'm the only one on a first-name basis."

"Right. Trevor." Sabrina shook her head with a chuckle. "Guess I'm going to have to remember my own rules in addition to yours."

"I'll let you do her other side on your own," he said. "Once you're finished, we'll hose her down and towel her dry."

Trevor moved into the back room to get the right hose head. When he stepped back out, he paused in the doorway to watch Sabrina. She had to rise up on the toes of her formerly pristine cowboy boots to reach Peggy's back, but the adventure coordinator would allow for no oversight. *That is going to be one clean horse,* Trevor mused as he rejoined them. *Can't imagine old Peg's ever been so spoiled in her life.*

He didn't take his eyes off the petite blonde as his hands worked to attach the spray nozzle to the hose. He had thought the constant sight of Sabrina Hearthstone traipsing around his ranch in her too-tight pants would distract him from his work. He wasn't sure he thought any differently about it, seeing her now—but he was willing to let it stand. For the moment.

"Here." He passed the hose to her. "Dial it back and let her get used to the temp before you spray her down fully."

"Are you sure this thing is on completely?" Sabrina squinted one eye and studied it. "Hang on, is the dial supposed to read going *this* way?"

There it was. The return to normalcy he needed, the challenge to his knowledge he had been holding his breath for all morning. Trevor didn't know whether to feel annoyed or relieved at its reappearance now.

"It's on the right way," he stated. He crossed his arms and shifted his weight to one hip. "You think I haven't done this multiple times a day for the better part of fifteen years?"

"I'm just *saying* that I'm pulling the trigger and can't get any water out." Sabrina held the hose out of the way when he reached for it. "Hey, will you give me a minute? I'm not trying to start a fight or anything, I'm just saying the safety reads 'off,' but no water's coming out! There's got to be a blockage somewhere."

Sabrina turned the nozzle toward her face to study it again as Trevor backed off. The reason for the lack of water flow hit him: he hadn't turned it on at the spigot. He wheeled away from her on his heel and fought the urge to slap his forehead at the oversight. *Not your fault,* he told himself internally as he crouched to twist the faucet on. *You're not used to having a woman around. You're distracted.*

A wild gasp of breath from behind him caused his head to swivel in alarm. Whatever had just happened to Sabrina, she had suppressed the instinct to scream to avoid startling Peggy. As it was, the mare was throwing her head back and yanking at the lead rope. Clearly *something* had spooked her while his back was turned.

"What is it?" He was on his feet and all but running to Sabrina's side. "Did she bite you? How are you hurt—?"

The adventure coordinator turned, face dripping and ice-blue eyes rounded in shock. "No! No, I'm fine. Honestly!" She gave a little laugh at her own expense and put her hands up. "It's totally my fault. I was aiming it right at myself when you...."

Trevor's gaze traveled downward to reassure for himself that she was fine, and stopped immediately at her chest. His look went no further.

Sabrina's eyes narrowed in confusion. "What? What is it?" She glanced down and soon saw for herself what the trouble was. Her white T-shirt was plastered against the front of her frame and transparent all the way down to her navel. Her bra and the swell of her breasts beneath it were in stark evidence.

The bra was such a blinding shade of hot pink he was surprised he hadn't noticed it through the shirt before, even when it was dry. The shirt was such an ineffective buffer against the outside world now that he could have reached out and traced the lacework design through it with his finger, his whole hand....

Sabrina's chin shot up so quickly she probably gave herself whiplash. Only after her arms came up to cover herself was the spell over Trevor broken. He blinked and met her eyes. He had never seen a woman in more distress than his adventure coordinator.

"I..." she stammered. "Um..."

"Wait there."

For once she listened to him. Trevor snatched his Carhartt off the stable door and whipped it around her shoulders. The jacket was almost big enough to engulf her, and she closed it over herself gratefully.

"Thank you," she said after a moment. "Looks like my other shirt didn't escape the torrent, either." She gazed forlornly at the wet heap her flannel had become.

"This probably wasn't a good idea," Trevor mentioned.

"No," she agreed with a laugh. She reached out to pat Peggy's neck. Trevor noticed that Sabrina struggled to meet his eyes after the...incident...but he felt a similar aversion to looking at her, so he didn't press it.

"You want to go get changed, I'll finish up here with Peggy," he offered. "And I'll get you a list of tasks our guests could do around the ranch that might be a little less risky."

"A list would be nice," Sabrina said.

Trevor's mouth quirked. "You're going to wish you never said that."

"I have a feeling you're right!" Sabrina laughed. She raised her blue eyes from limbo to finally meet his, and her beatific smile he was already growing used to returned. "Thank you, Trevor." Sabrina stepped away from Peggy, closer to him. Her slender hand found his shoulder and she gave it a squeeze of gratitude. "At the very least, thank you for not giving me a hard time about all this. I promise I won't run into any more learning curves."

Coincidentally, *curves* were also on the forefront of Trevor's mind as he watched Sabrina turn and stride quickly from the stable. The addition of the Carhartt certainly left much to the imagination. Fortunately, Trevor now had a very clear image of the dips and swells of Sabrina Hearthstone's body, which he could recall any time he wished.

"I'm in trouble," he muttered. "Aren't I, Peg?"

Peggy rocked her head up and down and snorted.

Chapter 4
SABRINA

"All right, Sabrina," Sabrina whispered to herself. "You can do this."

A week and several of Trevor's lengthy checklists later, and she found herself striding across the dewy front lawn of Wildhorse about to address her first group of "visitors" to the ranch. The program was still in the testing phases, of course, which was why she had asked Trevor's help in gathering together some of the locals to try out a schedule of activities.

That was partly why she felt so nervous as she drew close to the group of people assembled in the driveway. City folks out of their element and looking to *her* for advice on how to have a good time? She could handle them. But these people were *locals:* tanned, rangy, and unlikely to be fazed by a single thing she had to say to them. They probably knew more about the activities they were about to participate in than she did, so it was up to her to put a unique spin on the proceedings and make them as fresh and enjoyable as possible.

The heels of her boots crunched across the gravel as she approached them. They all turned to look at her, and she did a quick head count. Ten. *Not bad at all, Trevor,* she approved privately as she stopped short in front of them and held her arms out.

"Hello, glampers!" she greeted them all with a cheery smile.

A hand shot up in the crowd, slicing through her introduction like a knife. Sabrina blinked. She hadn't counted on fielding participant questions this early—that was, immediately—but she knew how to roll with the punches. She retired her clipboard to her hip, broadened her smile encouragingly, and pointed into the crowd. "Yes? You in the back, did you have a question?"

"What's a 'glamper'?" the woman asked.

"It ain't a real word," the older man beside her provided. "It's one of those newfangled words, like 'selfie'."

"Well, that's…I'm so glad you asked that question, actually!" Sabrina stated, hoping the boisterous volume of her voice would be enough to drown out any further answers from those who sought to be helpful. "'Glamping' combines two words: 'glamorous' and 'camping'. We've all gathered here this week to experience life on a ranch as—"

"Wait, we're going to be doing this for a whole week?" someone else piped up. "Trevor said you only needed us for the afternoon."

"Yes. I apologize." Sabrina's smile didn't budge an inch. "I appreciate that you folks were kind enough to volunteer your time as stand-ins for me this afternoon. Please excuse me if I lapse into my normal monologue; our future guests will be vacationing with us much longer."

A ripple of conversation went through the small crowd. She could have sworn she heard the word "vacation" echoed several times in varying tones of disbelief. Her cheeks heated a little, but she kept her posture straight. Of course, the locals wouldn't understand the more charmed aspects of the existences they led from day-to-day—but maybe, just maybe, she could give them a new, glamorous perspective on their normal lives.

"Howdy, Trevor," one of the men on the fringe of the crowd called. Sabrina's heart stumbled, and she turned to see Trevor strolling down the driveway from the main house. His strides were relaxed and easy, and maybe even the slightest bit bowlegged, but he carried himself with an undeniable sexiness that was enough to stop her in her tracks. Trevor halted beside her, and the next part of the monologue she had prepared all but flew from her mind.

Should have made a checklist, Sabrina thought ruefully. *There's no way you'll get back on track now with Trevor Wild standing beside you.*

"Mornin' folks. Mornin', Sabrina," the rancher greeted her. God, she loved the way he rolled her first name around every inch of his mouth.

Wait, did she really just think that? She didn't have the spare brain power to devote to this right now! She was already off to a rocky start, and she needed to make every subsequent word to these people count.

"Thank you for joining us, Mister…*Trevor,*" she quickly corrected. She thumbed through the papers on her clipboard, even though there was nothing in the schedule she needed to check. She had everything memorized already. The fact that Trevor was standing so close, looking so good, made it difficult for her to function normally.

"So today, glampers, we're going to start you off small," Sabrina began again, adding an extra layer of cheer. "If you'd be so good as to follow me out to the west stable block—" She indicated the direction with a sweep of her hand, but found the group had already turned as one and started off. "Trevor has been so good as to set aside the smaller arena for our use. We're going to be watching one of our ranch hands, Pete, join up with one of our newer horses.

"Join up?" one of the women echoed. Sabrina nodded.

"Yes…yes!" She hustled to keep at the head of the group, turning to walk backwards as she explained. "Allow me to address what I mean by that! The process of joining up with a horse is an imperative part of establishing a working, loving relationship with your horse. Horses are herd animals naturally, and mutual trust between a horse and their handler is a key ingredient to their safety and comfort. A display of dominance lets them know that there is a strong, protective personality watching over them. That allows the horse to relax a little."

Sabrina shot a tentative look toward Trevor. She didn't know what she was expecting—an enthusiastic thumb's up, maybe, for her grasp of the premise—but the rancher's stoic expression only gave way to the faintest of smiles. She would take it.

"I know what joining up is," the woman explained to her. "But why is this something you want us to watch?"

"Yeah! Joining up's boring," a younger boy beside her volunteered.

Sabrina was starting to feel the strain of the smile she would be holding all afternoon. "Well, I can guarantee you that most of our guests coming in from the city have never seen or even heard of it before. Heck, we may even get some visitors who have never seen a real live horse."

"That's stupid!" The boy chuckled.

"Not stupid. Just…different," Sabrina said as she steered him toward the fence. "Not everyone was as lucky as I was when I was a kid. I got to see horses every time I visited my grandparents."

As she spoke, she could feel Trevor's eyes on her. It wasn't the first time she found herself wondering what he thought about her take on things. Did he think she was naïve for thinking herself lucky? Did he secretly think this whole operation was doomed, and that no one would ever see things the way she did? Would she have to prove *him* wrong, on top of proving to everyone else in the group that their lives were filled with excitement and value that others would be willing to pay for?

Better not to think about it and to focus on the present.

"Hey, Pete." Sabrina waved to the ranch hand slung across the far side of the fence. He returned her gesture with a cool top of his hat. "Who do you have for us today?"

"This is Tex," Pete announced. He jerked his thumb toward the young quarter horse beside him, a gelding with a shiny chestnut coat. "Me and him, we're about to join up. Care to watch?"

"Do we have to?" one of the kids whined.

Yes! You have to! Sabrina wanted to shout. Instead, she redirected her aggressive energy into clutching her clipboard and smiling so hard her teeth ground together. *Trevor is counting on you,* she reminded herself. *Don't let him down.*

"All right, everyone, if you'll please look to the arena, Pete is about to begin his demonstration," she said. Pete nodded and vaulted into the dirt ring. The ranch hand moved to the center; as if on cue, Tex began to trot around the perimeter. Pete demonstrated how, with a few clicks of his tongue and motions with the unattached lead rope, he could get Tex to turn on a dime and start back the other way. Sabrina, who had never seen this sort of training herself, was enrapt with the easy communication between man and horse.

But her stand-in glampers were less enthused. Several of the men had doffed their hats and turned slightly away from the arena as they chatted about the weather; some of the women had their chins in their hands and appeared lost in even deeper discussion with one another.

Her patience snapped. "Everyone!" Sabrina shouted. "If you wouldn't mind keeping some of the chatter down, I'm sure Pete and Tex would *appreciate* your cooperation!"

"It's all right."

A gentling hand rested on her white-knuckled fist, and Trevor extracted the clipboard from her grip before she could splinter it. "It was a good idea. I think you should keep it. You're going to get different folks in and out of here, and all of them are going to react differently to the activities."

Sabrina blushed. It wasn't the first time she had the impression that Trevor was using his skills as a horseman to soothe her, but she appreciated the gesture more than she could say. As acutely aware as she was that much of Wildhorse's future relied on her and her program, she didn't feel so alone and solely responsible when Trevor stood this near to her.

She hung off the fence and sighed in momentary defeat. Trevor set her clipboard aside and joined her.

"I didn't know that," Trevor murmured quietly. "About your grandparents."

Maybe he was trying to take her mind off things. Sabrina watched Tex's gait speed to a loping canter, following Pete's wordless instruction, and waited until the horse had made another pass before replying. "I guess I didn't think it was important for you to know," she said. *I didn't think you'd be interested,* was her private thought.

"Where do they live now?" he asked her.

"Here."

He started a little, but Sabrina only shrugged. "It's part of why I took this job. They had to sell their ranch in Colorado when they retired. Now they live in a retirement community right outside of town. Which reminds me, I need to go visit them."

"Take whatever time you need," Trevor replied. "As long as you promise to actually take that time off and not spend it trying to come up with more of your ideas."

"Looks like I might have to," Sabrina said bitterly. She was looking at the faces arrayed around the arena fence. Their expressions ranged from politely interested, to bored, to mocking amusement at the display before them.

At least Pete was being a good sport about it. He continued to drive Tex around the ring, flicking his lead rope to redirect the horse's path. It was over all too quickly. Tex paused and angled himself toward the handler. Pete turned away, and the horse sauntered to join him in the center of the ring. One person clapped.

Sabrina would have hidden her face in her hands if she wasn't conscious that others might be watching. "Maybe we should skip the horse shoe decorating," she muttered.

Trevor winced. Sabrina would have liked to think it was because he would personally *miss* the horseshoe decorating, but she knew the man better. He took his hat off, settling it on her head. Sabrina blinked in surprise. The gesture was strangely affectionate, and she felt empowered despite her confusion.

"Whatever you decide, I'm here for you," he said as he turned back to the arena. Pete was now allowing the locals to take turns riding Tex bareback around the arena; most, including the young boy from earlier, were showing off various tricks they knew and laughing. "Just promise me you won't let this lot run you off screaming," Trevor continued.

You would know all about that, wouldn't you, Trevor? Sabrina thought rebelliously. *Considering you and your orneriness did your best to run me off first.*

Well, if she could get Trevor Wild to come around to her way of seeing things—no matter how rarely it happened—then maybe, just maybe, she stood a chance of actually getting through to these people.

After all, what else could possibly go wrong at this point?

*   *   *

After the "guests" had gone, Sabrina escaped to the easternmost stable block, where she and Trevor had bathed Peggy what felt like a lifetime ago. Who could have guessed that she, Sabrina Hearthstone, would prove a failure in every small lifetime Wildhorse had to offer her?

And whoever suspected that in her time of need, a box of sugar cubes would deliver itself as the ultimate comfort?

Even without a schedule of her secret comings and goings, Trevor found her. She sat dismally on a stool she had pulled up outside Peggy's stall, feeding the gentle horse sugar lump after sugar lump. The warm, snorting breaths and the tickle of lips as large as the palm of her hand had briefly provided the distraction she needed, but now that Trevor was strolling toward her in the gloom, even that wasn't enough.

"You girls eating your feelings?" he asked her. He stopped and leaned against the stall door; Peggy broke off from her candy feast briefly to acknowledge him, raising her snout to his shoulder and snorting in his scent. Sabrina dipped into the box in her lap and thrust a sugar-laden hand back through the door sullenly.

"Today was an unmitigated disaster," she reminded him, in case he was in danger of forgetting what a failure she was.

"No." A quiet, one-word protest.

"They were all laughing when they left," she said bitterly. "All of them. I also saw quite a few disbelieving headshakes. In case you didn't realize, that means our focus group was a complete bust."

"No, it doesn't," Trevor replied. "It just means that I stacked the odds against you. The folks you dealt with today have been doing ranch work since before they could walk. It's in their blood—a sort of genetic memory. They're set in their ways because it's more than chores or participation for them, it's tradition. Hell, I'm impressed you managed to stand your ground with the lot of them—and you can bet that you impressed them." Sabrina made a disbelieving noise in her throat, but Trevor crossed his arms and stood by his claim. "You might still be a puzzle to them, but they know tenacity when they see it. You earned their respect today, Sabrina."

"Fat lot of good that does me," Sabrina said, "and fat lot of good that does *you*. I appreciate you gathering up a group for me to work with, Trevor, but these aren't the people we'll be aiming to impress once the program's put in place. Maybe they're not easily won-over, but what about *paying* customers? What about the people who don't know you well enough to show up as a favor? They'll be expecting a fresh, out-of-this-world experience, and I…."

Sabrina trailed off. She wasn't so far gone in her own pity party not to understand that *I might not be the right person for this job* was trespassing into territory she didn't want either of them to consider. Even if she felt like she had let Trevor and the ranch down, she couldn't give up on them yet—no matter how much she might be considering their own best interests by doing so.

The rancher leaned down and caught her hand on its way back into Peggy's stall. "Enough," he said quietly. "You'll make her sick if you keep feeding her like that."

Sabrina felt her own face turn scarlet in shame. She allowed Trevor to pull her to her feet, and she handed him the box of sugar cubes. "Sorry. I wasn't thinking." Just one more failure to add to her ever-growing list, but at least giving Peggy a belly ache had been avoided, however narrowly.

"You've already spoiled her rotten," he continued his lecture as he set the box aside. "You should save that sort of attentiveness for the guests."

Amidst his instruction, Trevor kept hold of her hand. Sabrina leaned into him gratefully and rested her head against his shoulder. His silence had her suddenly second-guessing whether he had intended the gesture as one of comfort or had just forgotten where his hand was.

Sabrina made to pull away again, wondering if there was absolutely *anything* she could get right today, but the rancher surprised her by holding on.

"Come on." He wrapped his free arm around her waist and led her over to a hay bale where they could both sit—and out of reach of the horses, Sabrina noted. As if he didn't trust her to discontinue her sugar cube campaign. They sat down together, and he separated himself from her a little, but the muscled length of his jean-clad thigh still touched hers.

Trevor cleared his throat awkwardly after a moment. "So, things didn't go as planned," he summarized. "You stick with it, make a new plan. You try again."

"By 'plan,' don't you mean list?"

"If need be," he agreed. Sabrina rolled her eyes a little, but she couldn't help the grateful smile tugging at the edge of her lips.

Trevor shifted beside her, the material of his jeans catching against hers.

"Look," he went on, "I'm not in love with the changes you're making around here—but like it or not, the success of my operation depends on you. The *horses* are counting on you." He gestured down the aisle at the long, curious faces that poked out of their stalls occasionally to watch them. "The income from your program is buying us all time. Time for *me* to figure out how to get the breeding program back off the ground. Without time, I have to start selling off horses, and quarter horse breeding stock that doesn't do what it was bred to do could wind up anywhere, despite my best efforts to police their rehoming. I don't want to consider it, but it's the reality all the same."

"I guess I never thought of it that way," Sabrina admitted. "Now I feel even more pressure to make this work."

"We'll make this work," Trevor amended. "I don't want you to feel like the future of Wildhorse is all on your tiny shoulders." He grinned crookedly. "Doubt you could hold it there, anyway, what with those earrings already weighing you down."

"Well, I don't want you to feel alone in this, either," Sabrina replied. After a thoughtful pause, she laid a hand on his knee and looked up. "Even though I know it's probably worthless to argue that point," she added, the smile catching at her lips once more. "This is your whole life, Trevor. It's your home. I'm lucky you invited me into even a small part of it, and I promise I won't let you down."

"I know you won't." To her surprise, he brought his hand up once more to encase hers. His filth-encrusted work gloves hung from his belt, and the hand that held hers was large and rough and surprisingly warm. She remembered how he had grabbed hold of her hand earlier, and how she had thought it was a fluke—a thoughtless maneuver to steer her as he would one of his horses. Now, Sabrina thought it might be something different.

So, she took the same risk as earlier and laid her head on his shoulder. Her hair formed a comfortable cushion as she gazed out the open barn door toward the sprawling pastures. As much as she had insisted aloud that Wildhorse was Trevor's home, it already had a special place in her heart. For a woman who made her living and carved her own happiness by jetting from location to location, she always found the ease she felt in the country surprising.

And the ease she felt being this close to Trevor Wild might have also had something to do with her love of Wildhorse. How had they gone so quickly from being adversaries to allies? Granted, *collaboration* was something they had been working toward since the beginning of their acquaintance…even if they had struggled with it. A lot. Sabrina doubted it would be long at all before they were butting heads again, but at least she could rest here on his shoulder between rounds.

This time, he wrapped his arm around her waist and pulled her in close. They sat silently together, both lost in their own thoughts about how to move forward. But it was hard to keep her wheels turning when she could feel Trevor's breath on her hair. The hand on her waist never loosened, never relaxed; it cemented her to his side and held her securely in place. Could she break away if she wanted to? *Did* she want to? Ever?

The quiet intensity of his gaze was too much. Sabrina glanced away to study the front of his plaid shirt and was dismayed to find the collar open.

In the next moment, his fingers caught her chin and lifted her face back up to him. The intensity hadn't left his eyes, but there was faint surprise in them, as if he had seen something unexpected in her expression and wanted to reassure himself that he hadn't imagined it. How could she hope to hide anything from him when he was this close?

Her eyes flickered to his lips, and she felt a tug of intense longing in her stomach. As if she had signaled him, Trevor leaned in—

And a wet, snuffling horse nose thrust itself between them.

"Peggy," Trevor groaned. "How the hell did you get out?"

"She's smart," Sabrina offered with a breathless little laugh. She pushed back against the interceding horse, and Peggy ducked her head to riffle Sabrina's pockets with her lips. *Not the lips I was planning to have on me a moment ago,* Sabrina thought with no small amount of disappointment. She took care to keep her eyes off Trevor as she grappled with the overly-friendly horse. Already she could feel herself second-guessing the moment.

There was no way Trevor Wild had been about to kiss her—right? There was no way she had been about to *let* him—right?

"She knows now you're the goose that lays the golden egg," Trevor said in a tone of mild disapproval. He heaved himself up from the hay bale and looped his arm around Peggy's neck, leading the obedient horse back to her stall without a halter.

Wildhorse's financial problems came flooding back to her, and Sabrina's eyes narrowed in determination. "Let's hope she's not wrong about that."

Chapter 5
TREVOR

"Where the *hell* did you get these?" Trevor demanded.

Things were back to normal between the ranch owner and his adventure coordinator a few days later. They currently stood together outside her cabin staring at the formidable scrap heap Sabrina had managed to pile up while he was out mending a fence that morning.

Trevor took his hat off and rubbed his scalp in dismay. "What is all this? It looks like a goddamned funeral pyre. Please tell me you aren't upcycling a jungle gym. A kid could get tetanus just by looking at this mess." He indicated the mangled iron bed frames with a point of his hat.

"Aren't they beautiful?" Sabrina enthused. She was either completely oblivious to the moody storm cloud he had brought in with him from the field or was deliberately ignoring it. He wasn't sure which irritated him more, to be frank. "I found them in the junkyard just across the street. Pete let me borrow his truck to bring them in, since you were out with yours." She ran a finger along the iron tracery of a half-intact frame. "I'm going to use them in the bedrooms—once they're all pieced together and finished, anyway. These will make perfect king-size headboards for all the beds. I think these will add *just* the right touch of romance that's been lacking so far in our glampers' accommodations. Glad I got up early!" She concluded with a joyful—and he suspected slightly over-caffeinated—laugh.

As always, Trevor found Sabrina's elaborate plans hard to follow. What he had no trouble zeroing in on was her claim of a junkyard. "What do you mean you went across the street?" he asked her slowly.

"Oh, come on." Sabrina attempted to wave off his question. "If you have a problem with me leaving the property during billable hours, you should have said so in one of your many, many lists, and I could have won this argument sooner."

"What I have a problem with is you trespassing on the neighbors' land!" Trevor exploded. "That property across the street is *not* a junkyard!"

"Sure it is!" Sabrina exclaimed. "The one with the busted old mailbox? It's obviously an unplumbed gold mine for upcyclers like me. I'm doing them a favor by dragging one or ten old bedframes off their hands!"

Trevor needed a moment to compose himself before he elaborated on her grave mistake, and a buzz from his back pocket provided him with the perfect distraction. He cursed under his breath and turned away. He would let Sabrina temporarily think she had won their argument as he read the text from his brother.

Hey, so you know, the Millers called the station earlier. Said some property of theirs has gone missing. Something about beds? Don't be surprised if Old Mrs. Miller leaves her hovel and comes asking about it.

"Do you..." Trevor struggled to get the words out. He slid his phone back into his pocket, text unanswered, and fought to keep his breathing even. "Do you have any idea what you've just done?" he finally managed.

Sabrina cocked her head at him. "You know, you weren't this dramatic about the wood pile," she mentioned. "What gives?"

"That 'unplumbed gold mine' you claim to have discovered is the Miller family's private *residence!*" he hissed through his teeth. "The Millers are hoarders, Sabrina, and infamous throughout Lockhart Bend for their situation. My brother just informed me that they put a call into the sheriff's office to report their property stolen!"

"Well...I'm happy to help them clean up their yard a bit by taking any unwanted items off their hands," Sabrina stated. "And if they want this stuff back, I'll load the truck up again and drive it back over there. All I have to do is offer an explanation, right? I'll apologize for my mistake, let them know I'm new to town. Heck, I might even take the opportunity to pass out a few fliers while I'm over there—"

"Are you even listening to me?" Trevor shouted. "The police report's already been filed! Do you think I have any free time to deal with this today? Odds are I'll have to drag you over there and sort this thing out and *hope* that having a sheriff brother counts for something!"

Sabrina waved a dismissive hand at him. "Trent will understand. It was all a misunderstanding," she repeated. "And anyway, I thought you would appreciate my efforts to recycle. All the rental cabins are in desperate need of a makeover. I was only trying to save you money, and save *you* the hassle of worrying about where those furnishings would come from! A little support wouldn't go amiss!"

Trevor growled at her response. He couldn't help his own temper, and he sure as hell didn't appreciate her trying to turn the tables on him and make *him* the bad guy, considering *he* wasn't the one implicated in a goddamned robbery. He yanked his work gloves off and slapped them against his thigh, just for something to hit; they tracked a dirt smear on his already filthy Wranglers.

"You know why I really think you're mad?" Sabrina continued suddenly, unexpectedly. Her blue eyes narrowed as she scrutinized him, and Trevor didn't think he liked this shift, not one bit. "I think you're mad because you took a peek at my reservation list and saw that your ex-girlfriend is currently occupying the top slot."

"Who the hell told you about Marcy?" he demanded. It was futile to claim at this point that he *hadn't* looked, but Marcy had nothing to do with this...*this*....

"She did," Sabrina stated defiantly. "She told me she felt awkward booking a reservation but wanted to show her support for Wildhorse and the new program. That's why she specifically asked for one of the remoter cabins on the property—which, it so happens, is in dire need of a new bed. Please don't tell me you intend to sabotage your *own* program just because you—"

"Because I what?" Trevor interrupted.

Sabrina expelled a sigh of frustration and threw up her hands. "Because you still have feelings for her!" she exclaimed. "There, I said it! Marcy and I both tiptoed around your past relationship while we were on the phone together, but she obviously felt comfortable enough with the idea of being here that she was the first to book an overnight!"

"You think I have feelings for Marcy?" he growled. "You think *that's* why you and I are fighting? If that's the case, then you've already lost this round."

"I don't think I've lost anything!" Sabrina persisted. "In fact, I don't see you offering up anything in the way of proof that I'm completely, totally wrong in my—"

Trevor dropped his gloves and hat and seized her around the waist. Sabrina broke off in shock as he pulled her in against him. Her hands flew to his chest, but there was no warding off his advance, his indomitable strength. They collided at the hips, and before Sabrina could draw another breath, the rancher swooped in and put a stop to her words—catching her chin between his thumb and forefinger, he kissed her.

Kissing Sabrina in a fit of passion banished thoughts of any other woman completely. Those soft, pink lips that drove him crazy practically any time they parted to speak now parted against his mouth in a breathless gasp. Sabrina slipped her arms around his neck, and Trevor advanced seamlessly into the next stage at her signal. What had started as a tactic to shut her up, to prove to her just how over Marcy he was, had escalated without his consent in the matter—and he wouldn't have it any other way. Their near-miss in the barn after the first glamping trial had nagged at him ever since.

Now he knew what he had been missing. Trevor drew her harder against him, and she came unresisting, her fingers clutching at the dark crop of his hair. His tongue swept along the voluptuous curve of her bottom lip. She tasted warm and safe, like the brand of coffee he'd favored since his first taste of the stuff. He slipped his tongue past her lips, past the perfect teeth that formed that perfect, ambitious smile, and Sabrina moaned quietly against him. His tongue slid along the length of hers, parrying each thrust. If she intended to drive him out, she underestimated his commitment to winning their argument...

If only he could remember what the terms were.

When he had satisfied himself, Trevor withdrew, expelling a hot gasp as he went. Sabrina lingered in his arms and rested her forehead against his chin. After filling the property with their raised voices for the last half hour, the yard felt strangely silent. Trevor wet his lips and was about to speak, but Sabrina beat him to the punch.

"Do you...want to come up to my cabin?" she asked him quietly.

*   *   *

I really shouldn't be doing this, Trevor thought as he ducked beneath the doorway of Sabrina's bunkhouse. *It's not even noon yet. Didn't I expressly tell her I don't have time for distractions today?*

But he was like a willingly broke horse on the other end of an invisible lead, and Sabrina was calling the shots. After a kiss like that, he would damn near follow her anywhere....

Sabrina moved into the kitchen to brew a fresh pot of coffee. He momentarily considered following her and putting any harried thought of hospitality to rest with a suggestive placement of his hands in a few choice spots along her trim little body…but he refrained. Like it or not, he could still summon the willpower to suppress most of his baser urges, even if Sabrina was making it harder by the day—in more ways than one. He hovered awkwardly by the kitchen's island, unsure if he should sit or stand. He finally settled on sitting. He pulled out a stool that was too small for his long legs and set his hat to the side. After a moment, Sabrina turned back around and placed a mug of coffee in front of him. He didn't reach for it immediately.

"So," she said.

"So."

"I'll return the bed frames," she offered.

"And I'll deal with Trent," Trevor said. "You want to wait around a bit, you can likely talk him into returning them for you. He has more experience dealing with the Millers, and if we explain the situation to him…well." He kicked at a loose floorboard with the toe of his boot. "He'll likely come up with something to get them to drop the charges. He's the type to bend the rules for a pretty face."

"Guess that's another thing you Wild brothers *don't* have in common," Sabrina said casually.

Trevor flushed. It wasn't with anger, exactly, but the intense heat she had aroused in him had to escape somewhere.

"Something on your mind?" he asked pointedly. He didn't want to do this dance with her. What were the odds of them returning to the way things were before, after a kiss like that? "If so, you should come out and say it," he continued. "I make my living playing by the rules. The success of this ranch and the lives tied to it *depend* on my rules. But that doesn't mean I feel the need to deny myself everything."

"That kiss…" Sabrina's lovely face lapsed into a faraway expression. Trevor studied it intensely. The eager way her mouth had moved against his only moments ago told him he wasn't the only one struggling with an attraction, but he wanted to hear her say it. "That kiss was something else," she arrived at finally. Her fingers clenched over her mug. "But I'm not sure we should repeat it."

In contrast, Trevor was damn sure they would.

"I mean, it's not that I didn't enjoy it. I really, *really* enjoyed it." She reached up to brush a disheveled strand of hair out of her eyes. "God, I feel like you're making me lose my mind."

"I'm making *you* lose your mind?" he repeated with a raised eyebrow.

Sabrina shook your head. "You're right. We have to stop clashing like this…and that's why I invited you here. I have an idea about how to defuse the situation."

Trevor had more than *one* idea on that front, and he was willing to spend the afternoon trying them all out on her. Forget the damn work schedule. His blood started pumping as she came around to his side of the bar. He was just about to take her in his arms and carry her into the back bedroom when she slapped a pamphlet down in front of him. Trevor blinked. After a moment, he shifted to get a better look at it.

"We'll deal with the bedframes, like you said," Sabrina said. "I'll fix my mistake—even though they would make *great* atmospheric décor and are only going to waste otherwise—and apologize to Trent and the Millers. And then I want us to try this out. As a team-building exercise."

"Team-building exercise?" Trevor tapped the brochure. "This is a riding competition."

Sabrina nodded. "Yeah. A *team* competition. Everyone who works here has to participate. And it's not only for the benefit of the ranch staff; the benefits will trickle down to our campers. We can take what we learn and our experience with the activities and find a way to apply those same activities and philosophies to our glamping program."

"And it was my kiss that inspired you to bring this up?" he asked, amused despite himself.

Sabrina blushed. "It might have tripped a light bulb. Or several. At the very least, it reminded me that we get a lot more accomplished when we're…in sync."

Trevor studied the curves of her body as she moved back into the tiny kitchen. He couldn't discuss business just yet—he was still lost in the memory of having her folded against him.

"This rodeo is down the road from here." Trevor set the pamphlet down and eased back in his stool, crossing one arm over the other. "Most of the hands participate in it every year anyway. Should be easy enough to get them behind the idea of forming a team, even if it isn't exactly billed as a team-building exercise."

Sabrina leaned across the counter and grinned. "So, you'll sign us up?" she said.

"And pay the entry fee, I assume," Trevor muttered.

"I'll pay the entry fee."

"Fine," he agreed. "We'll enter."

Sabrina gave a small cry of excitement; she leapt up and pumped her fist. A rare smile curved across Trevor's face. He reached across the counter to shake on it, and the moment Sabrina's fingers slipped inside his own, he gripped them tight. "On one condition," he added. "You're going to be *my* partner in the rescue race."

"The...rescue race?" Sabrina echoed. Her unfamiliarity didn't diminish her own smile. "What is that? Like a relay race?"

"You might call it that," he answered mysteriously as he rose. "Meet me in the arena at sunset. And wear some damn jeans you can ride in."

"And if I can convince the Millers to let me keep the bedframes?" she asked hopefully.

Trevor snorted. Fat chance of that, but he couldn't help relenting in the face of her optimistic expression. As he headed out the door, he caught sight of something hanging above the doorway. It was a five-pointed, silver star. After losing every argument, culminating in a kiss that proved a significant lapse in his self-control, he felt a sudden need to reassert some authority.

"At the very least take this down," he remarked as he reached for it. "We're not decorating for Christmas *this* early."

"No!" Sabrina lunged after him. The shrill, desperate quality to her voice stopped him dead in his tracks. He froze, hand hovering over the ornament. She spoke more calmly. "I'm sorry, it's just that...my grandfather gave that to me. It's important."

"Why is it important?" he asked curiously. He could tell by her tone that she wasn't lying. He gazed at her critically, but Sabrina did everything in her power not to meet his eyes.

"If we win the riding competition...then I'll tell you," she promised. "But *only* if we win."

"Then I expect you to be out at the arena promptly this evening," he said. "Before sundown," he added over his shoulder as he shoved the door open. "That's at seven—"

"Seven-thirty. I know." Sabrina smiled ruefully and pointed toward her refrigerator. "You made a list about it, remember? I know when the sun sets, down to the minute, every single day for the next three months."

Trevor nodded in approval. He replaced his hat atop his head and started back across the lawn, skirting the pile of iron frames that had pried open this can of worms. *If only the Millers knew the damn mess they've inspired around here. They'd sure as hell be proud,* he mused.

The memory of Sabrina's lips preoccupied him for the rest of the work day. More than once, he found a horse shying from him or a tool slipping out of his grasp due to his errant thoughts.

He couldn't shake the impression that Sabrina had purposefully distracted him with the riding competition. He wondered if she had needed time to get her own thoughts about what had happened between them in order. *He* sure as hell couldn't claim to know what the next step was.

Guess we'll find out one way or another, he mused. He rose from his last task of the day and wiped the sweat from his brow. The gloves came off, and he slapped the dust off them against the outside of his thigh as he looked off toward the horizon. The sun sank slowly towards the distant hills, casting the Texas skyline in a ruby-red hue that darkened to a glorious amber the closer evening crept.

Trevor replaced his hat. Then he started toward the arena.

CHAPTER 6
SABRINA

Sabrina spent all afternoon Googling what a "rescue race" was. By the time she reunited with Trevor that evening, she had a pretty good grasp of what all it entailed.

She wasn't sure whether to be thrilled or terrified.

"So, it starts with a team of two people," Trevor began as he roped in Pete—figuratively—for a demonstration. Trevor walked out into the dirt arena leading a saddled Tex beside him. "Three, if you're counting the horse. The 'rescuer' is the first rider and gets let out of the gate at the start of the run. The rider meets up with the 'damsel' on the other side of the ring."

Pete, who Sabrina suspected had begun drinking as soon as his shift was over, dropped a curtsey and giggled as girlishly as his baritone would allow. Sabrina rolled her eyes. She stayed by the fence, though—despite the ease exhibited by the two men, she knew what was coming next.

Trevor swung up into the saddle and steered Tex toward the starting point. "The rider comes in breakneck—as fast as the two partners are comfortable with. Winning teams gallop!" he hollered over to her as he turned around and suddenly spurred

Tex into a sprint. The quarter horse lunged across the arena toward Pete.

Sabrina had never seen Trevor ride before. The way the rancher carried himself astride his saddle winded her almost as much as his speed did. She watched the surging motion of the horse and the way Trevor's hips rocked forward into the saddle; he almost appeared to hover above his seat, motionless, even as he leaned his long body dangerously far out over Tex's neck.

"We ride up!" he continued, shouting so she could hear him over the drumming of hooves. "Slow up! Take a sharp turn. Soon as I'm around…"

Sabrina held her breath. Trevor pulled Tex around Pete, and the ranch hand—without so much as a visible flinch to get out of the way of the thundering horse—reached up and grasped Trevor's outstretched arm. Trevor hauled the other man up onto the back of the saddle, and they bolted off together toward the starting point and a sliding stop.

The two men trotted over to her. Sabrina strained herself upright and clapped desperately, overwhelmed.

"Of course, it will go a lot faster with a tiny thing like you on back," Pete said as he swung himself down again.

Tex danced a little beneath Trevor, and the rancher reached down to give the horse a solid pat of approval. "I'm going to run him back and forth a few more times. He needs to burn off some excess energy before I can get him to start heeding me on the turn. Then you're up, Sabrina," he warned as he trotted off.

Sabrina swallowed audibly. She wasn't sure she had what it took not to break for the fence screaming with a ton of horseflesh and steel-shod hooves bearing down on her. "You guys look like you've done this before," she mentioned once she found her voice again.

Pete hung off the fence beside her. "Trevor's always been damn good at the rescue race," he remarked with a low whistle. "He and Marcy used to practice for it together, but they broke up by the time the next competition rolled around. Nice to see he found his inspiration again."

Sabrina's eyes narrowed at the figure trotting around the arena. *And just what inspiration is that?* she wondered. She couldn't help the way Marcy's name lingered in her brain. She even had an extremely positive conversation with the other woman earlier that week....

Was she actually starting to feel jealous?

"Hold my earrings," she muttered, unhooking the silver horseshoes and thrusting them into Pete's hand.

"These things are earrings?" she heard him ask in astonishment, but she was already over the top of the fence and heading across the arena to her designated damsel position. Trevor pulled Tex up and raised an eyebrow; he seemed surprised to see her taking the initiative.

"You ready to give it a go?" he asked. "I'll walk him the first few times until you're comfortable."

"Oh, I'm comfortable all right!" Sabrina replied, with a little too much enthusiastic volume in her voice. "You boys come at me as fast as you want!" She punched her fist into the palm of her hand. "Let's get this rescue ride on the road!"

If Trevor suspected her of acting strangely, well—he probably thought it was nothing *that* far out of the ordinary. The rancher turned and spurred Tex to the other end of the arena. Before she had a moment to steel her courage and maybe really *think* about what she was about to do, the horse came galloping back toward her.

She was *so* not ready for this.

She threw her arms up at the last instant and clenched her eyes tightly shut as Tex came barreling past her. Somehow, they had managed to avoid a collision. She coughed and waved her hand in front of her face as the cloud of dust settled.

"Good girl." Trevor reined Tex around in front of her and grinned. "You didn't move from that spot. Consider your first test a pass."

"Because I *trusted* you!" Sabrina seethed. "You were trying to freak me out on purpose!

"Because you *do* trust me," Trevor corrected her. "Whether you like it or not. I would never hurt you, Sabrina." The tightness around his dark brown eyes softened, and Sabrina's heart gave a little flutter at the expression he fixed her with. "But now you know what to expect when we actually get out there and compete. I don't expect you to be on Pete's level right off the bat. We'll work our way up, and you'll surpass him in no time. I promise we'll take it a bit slower this go-round."

Sabrina cast a helpless glance over to where Pete stood, but the ranch hand was fiddling with her earrings and completely oblivious to the action unfolding in the arena.

There was no one to rescue her but Trevor Wild—and she wasn't certain he wouldn't trample her in the attempt.

*   *   *

"You almost made it up that time!" Trevor shouted as he trotted off. "One more!"

"You've been saying 'one more' for the last *fifty* minutes," Sabrina moaned. She was tired, hot, and thirsty, and moths the size of small birds fluttered around the arena's lights. The night sky beyond the practice ring was a dark velvet blue, the winking white stars that dotted it all that kept it from going completely black. What time was it, anyway? Pete was long gone, and she suspected he had left with her earrings.

Worse than her exhaustion was the fact that she hadn't been able to take her mind off kissing Trevor. She had *thought* she had enough alone time with her thoughts for her feelings to develop into a full-blown infatuation with the rugged rancher, but his bullheadedness now was casting *those* feelings into extreme doubt. *What the hell did I ever see in this asshole?* she wondered as he came barreling back toward her. *Besides the chiseled face and the dark, dreamy bedroom eyes I mean. Besides the fact that he's tall and good-looking and good with his hands. Besides the fact that he's the strong, silent type to a T, until he takes it into his head to make my life a living—*

Trevor drove Tex around her, and Sabrina reached instinctively for his outstretched hand. He clasped her arm and pulled her up behind him; she had just managed to get her foot in the stirrup he had freed up for her, when her purchase slipped. She fell backward with a cry of dismay and landed hard in the dirt.

"Might as well get someone in here to draw a chalk outline," she muttered as she reached back to rub her bruised tailbone. "I'm pretty sure my ass has landed in this exact spot the last ten times we tried this."

"You've made it up onto the horse plenty more times than that," Trevor reminded her. He pulled Tex up short and slid from the saddle. "You're a good rider. Wouldn't know it to look at you. You've got to hold onto me until we reach the finish."

Sabrina snorted. She accepted his outstretched hand and got to her feet.

"You seem distracted," he added. He kept hold of her hand even when she made a move to draw it back. "You're too tense on the pick-up. I need you to relax more."

"Yeah?" she countered. "I seem to recall you saying the same thing about Tex earlier. You gonna ride me around the arena to blow off some steam?"

"You shouldn't talk like that," he growled as he pulled her in against him. "I might take you up on it."

And just like that, the lips she had been fantasizing about all day were hers once more. Trevor swept her up in his arms and kissed her in such a perfect collision that it was hard to imagine they had ever been two opposing forces. It was harder still to imagine that he had ever *stopped* kissing her out by the bunkhouse. He picked up exactly where they had left off, and Sabrina was all too happy to renew their choreography.

But familiarity with the moves didn't put a damper on the exploration—if anything, it made it all the more exciting. Trevor knew exactly how to mold his lips against hers and how long to hold that electric pressure; he knew *exactly* when to pull back to change it up and start all over again. Soon she was more breathless in his arms than she had been getting the wind knocked out of her moments ago. Her knees quaked, and she clung to his shoulders. When she felt the first teasing flick of his tongue, she nearly came undone. The memory of what he could do with it whispered across the back of her brain like a password and she opened her mouth to him.

Trevor groaned and shifted himself closer dropping Tex's reins. Suddenly his hands were all over her, sliding up her waist, bunching the fabric of her bubblegum flannel shirt. His fingers found the small of her back and flared along the curve. Sabrina relished the sweep of his tongue, drawing it deeper inside of her, but she still felt unfulfilled. She *needed* him to claim every inch of her, inside and out, if she had any hope of curbing the wildfire the man from Wildhorse had stoked in her.

Trevor's hands retreated, and his mouth inevitably followed. Sabrina strained a little on her tiptoes in half-hearted chase, but his fingers caught her chin to stop her. "Maybe..." His voice was a husky whisper that sent thrills her. "Maybe you just needed a little *inspiration*."

"Maybe you're right." She twined her arms around his neck, her heart racing as fast as Tex's hooves. "If I'm relegated to playing the 'damsel,' maybe I need help getting into character."

"You can trust me, Sabrina," Trevor whispered. "If you give up control, and give yourself over to me—just like that—I promise I won't let you fall."

"I know you won't." She flushed and looked at the deep V of his collar.

"Give your instincts free rein," he murmured quietly. "You can do this. I know you can. You don't even have to think about it anymore. Just let your body—" Trevor's hands moved back down her slender waist and took hold of her by the hips—"move how it wants to." He rocked her gently back and forth, simulating the roughness of the ride.

It was the single sexiest motivational speech Sabrina had ever heard, and she would have liked nothing more than to interpret it in all the wrong ways. The moment ended too soon. Trevor's hands slid from her a second time, and the rancher turned to jog off and get hold of Tex once more. Sabrina touched her aching lips, but the pressure applied by her finger pads wasn't enough. It reminded her only fleetingly of how it had felt to let Trevor Wild kiss her.

"Coming back at you!" he called out to her. He swung himself up into the saddle and loped Tex back to the start gate. "You ready?"

"Ready!" she shouted breathlessly. Her body sang with adrenaline, but this time it was a wonderful rush. She felt no fear, no reservation as man and horse galloped toward her. What had once seemed to her like a tangle of legs and hard, deadly hooves, now seemed easier to follow. The world slowed.

It was all familiar. It was all choreography. She could map her team's movements the same way she mapped Trevor's kisses. When his hand reached down to her, she took it and gave control away.

Trevor hauled her up onto the saddle behind him. The moment he let her go to seize hold of the reins with both hands, Sabrina's own hands shot out to grasp his belt buckle and hold on. The three of them completed the turn together and took off back toward the gate.

She didn't know they had made it all the way back until Trevor was sliding off the saddle. He reached up to pull her down with him.

"Did we...did we do it?" she asked breathlessly. She cracked one eye open as soon as she touched the ground. Trevor yanked his hat off and threw it down between his boots. When he wheeled back around to face her, he wore a wide, elated smile— the first she had ever seen out of him.

"Are you kiddin' me?" he exclaimed. "We crushed it! That's the fastest I've ever pulled off a pickup! You repeat that performance, and I think we've got ourselves a winning team here!"

"No way. No way!" Sabrina barely knew if she was protesting or agreeing with him. The rancher's ecstasy was contagious. Her spirits soared even higher when he held his arms out to her. She flew to him without hesitance, without thought. She leapt into his open arms and wrapped her legs around his waist. One of his arms came down immediately to cradle her ass; the other hand slid up into her hair.

For once, the damsel was taking firm charge of her own rescue. She crushed her lips against his, enjoying the hard-packed muscle she could feel tightening between her clenched legs. Trevor's fingers flared possessively around her posterior. *Who's complaining about my jeans now?* Sabrina thought wickedly, before all thoughts vanished completely from her brain. Once again, she was on fire inside his arms.

Trevor turned them around and thrust her up against the closed gate. He took hold of both her thighs; now that her weight was better distributed, he moved his hips in a slow, steady rhythm against her own. She didn't even think he was aware that he was doing it, but the friction nearly drove Sabrina out of her mind with need. Now the tightness of her jeans was working in *her* favor, letting her feel through the thin designer denim just how little remained between their desperately joined bodies.

Tex whinnied beside them. Trevor paid no attention, but Sabrina really didn't want their current session to end with another wet horse nose thrust between them. She broke from their kiss and pushed Trevor's shoulder to keep him at bay as she spoke. "Let's shut the lights down and put Tex up in the barn," she suggested.

Trevor gazed back at her wordlessly. His dark eyes were hooded, as if she had only managed to half-rouse him from the dream he found himself in. He let her down slowly, reluctantly.

"We won," she reminded him as she snatched up Tex's reins.

"Yeah," Trevor agreed. His eyes followed her in the darkness as she let herself out the gate. "But we still weren't anywhere near close to crossing that finish line."

They hadn't been back in the stable for more than a minute before Sabrina felt a pair of hands seize her waist.

"Hey!" she protested. She dropped Tex's reins in surprise as Trevor maneuvered her out of the aisle. A clumsy, calamitous half-second later, and the rancher had thrust *her* into the freshly-cleaned stall instead of his horse.

"You don't get off that easily," he stated. He herded her back toward the shadows of the wall, and Sabrina allowed herself to be cornered. She couldn't help the breathless laugh of excitement that escaped her.

"Well, neither do you…apparently," she teased him in turn. Trevor pinned her wrists above her head and leaned in.

"You have no idea what you do to me," he growled into the hollow of her throat.

"What...about...Tex?" she managed to gasp between heaving breaths.

Trevor freed one hand only long enough to shove the stall door closed behind him. "Don't worry about him. He knows when to stay put and follow orders...unlike some."

Sabrina wondered if she had awakened a side of Trevor even more domineering than his daytime personality. The thought probably shouldn't have excited her as much as it did. The heady scent of fresh hay and the claustrophobic darkness only heightened her awareness of him. They were both sweaty, filthy, and disheveled from drilling in the arena, but Sabrina had never felt more alive. The unbearable tension that had existed between them since they first met seemed about to fulfill its promise.

Trevor's teeth grazed along the vulnerable flesh of her neck. Sabrina raised her hips off the wall, and he pushed back forcefully. "The way you wrapped your legs around me in the arena..." he whispered. He trailed his lips up to her ear.

"You're the one who said I was a good rider," she retorted. "And what else did you say? Oh, right." She brushed her cheek against his and breathed his own words back into his ear. "But you 'wouldn't know it to look at me.'"

"I knew you were the most beautiful woman I had ever seen the moment I laid eyes on you," he whispered into her hair. The compliment stunned Sabrina, and for a moment she forgot how to be clever. As if sensing his small victory, Trevor took advantage of the moment and cemented himself against her fully. "Anyone with a pair of working eyes would," he continued. "But I can't speak to any prowess otherwise. Not yet."

He was referencing her *riding* skills yet again, and the double entendre crossing the lips of a man who seemed to pride himself in his lack of spontaneity and imagination sent a dark shiver through her. She couldn't get over seeing this sexually awakened side of Trevor, and she doubted that she would want to any time soon.

"You've kissed me, haven't you?" she whispered against his lips. "I think you should have some idea of this city girl's prowess by now."

"Not nearly enough of an idea," he growled. He took her mouth in a kiss that silenced any further sass, and pressed her back once more into the shadows.

Keeping her breathing anywhere near regular, with Trevor Wild doing the things he was doing to her now, proved impossible. She gasped and clutched the back of his neck as she felt his broad, warm hands slide up beneath her shirt. He thrust his tongue between her teeth in the same instant he pushed her underwire out of his way. His rough, strong fingers forked and caught her nipples between them. He massaged the hills of her breasts, gripping and pushing until it was almost painful, but Sabrina relished his force. Her nipples tightened with arousal, and Trevor groaned into her mouth. The pads of his fingers stroked and teased the pebbled flesh until Sabrina thought she would come undone. She writhed and bucked off from the wall, but he pinned her firmly with his hips and redoubled his pressure.

The sensation his exploration invoked was almost too good to put words to. Trading passionate kisses was one thing, but having Trevor feeling her up beneath her shirt kicked this thing between them up a notch. She had almost been able to fool herself that there was nothing between them—that the kisses were a way to vent their frustration, another item in the argument toolkit and nothing more—but her heart was almost leaping into the palm of his hand now with excitement.

There was no going back from this. She wanted him, and Trevor wanted her just as badly. He was going to have her, right here and now. He owned every inch of Wildhorse, and now he owned every inch of her.

One of his hands detached from her breast to slip down her stomach and past the waistband of her pants. Sabrina broke away and gasped wildly as he pressed into the heat between her legs.

"Tex? What are you still doin' out?" Pete's voice inquired.

Sabrina's hand flew to her mouth to stifle any further noise. The stable hand had entered the barn, but he didn't appear to realize they were still there. Trevor crowded her back further into the shadows to keep them both out of sight as Pete took it upon himself to unsaddle the horse, muttering all the while. He led Tex into the empty stall across from theirs and closed him in for the night; he departed as quickly as he had come, turning the lights off as he went.

"I don't pay that man enough," Trevor remarked as he turned back to Sabrina. She saw his eyes flash and quickly put her hands out to stop him from resuming their activity.

"Trevor, this isn't a good idea," she whispered. As she mentally wrestled for a reason why, the rancher pressed his hand more firmly between her legs until she saw stars. She cried out and grabbed for his wrist quickly. "I mean it!" she exclaimed. "What if Pete goes looking for you? What if he comes back? I definitely don't want someone I work with to find us in…find us doing…."

She couldn't find the word she wanted, but Trevor seemed to know what she meant. He groaned in defeat and slumped against her, the bulge in his jeans pressing against her leg. He breathed raggedly against her neck, and for a moment Sabrina wanted to take back everything she had just said and let him have his way with her. He wasn't the only one having difficulty turning off what they had started.

But she knew she needed to give her head a chance to catch up with her body. She needed time to remind herself what her priorities were before diving headfirst into this…this pulse-pounding, electric *thing* that kept rearing up between them at inopportune moments.

"I'll walk you back to your cabin," Trevor offered once he had collected himself.

Sabrina wanted nothing more than for him to accompany her back across the moonlit property, which was exactly how she knew what her answer had to be.

"No," she murmured. "I can walk myself." She reached up to grasp the back of his neck lightly, fleetingly. "See you tomorrow for practice?"

Trevor turned his head away in the darkness, and she read it as assent. She didn't blame him for feeling disappointed. She had never felt so unfulfilled in all her life, and she only had herself to blame.

Her voice of reason better have a *damn* good reason for keeping Trevor Wild at arm's length. Otherwise, there was no telling how she might decide to consummate this latest aspect of their partnership—but she had a feeling her body would be the one taking the reins.

Chapter 7
TREVOR

Things were awkward with his adventure coordinator, even now, on the day of the competition, when they should have been concentrating on their ride. Despite both their efforts to keep appearances up, Trevor knew no one on Team Wildhorse could mistake the tension that simmered below the surface of every little interaction between them—and every major argument.

"Trevor, for the last time, *no* I did *not* bring a change of jeans, so these are going to have to suffice!" Sabrina exclaimed.

Trevor didn't think the blonde could drive her fists into her hips any harder if she tried. His own body language was likewise broadcasting his discontent; his crossed arms and squared shoulders made him a formidable figure, but Sabrina didn't appear to notice his signals for her to back down.

"And for the record," she continued, "I don't appreciate you fashion-policing me in front of our teammates!"

She wasn't doing much herself to keep their argument private. Pete, Lorne, and Rodrigo all openly exchanged looks. The five of them were gathered along the outermost fence line of the arena, near where their team's designated area had been set up.

The small rodeo—which featured locals and their own mounts, rather than bulls and broncos off the circuit—was held every year on Frank Buckton's property, which was about five times bigger than Wildhorse Ranch. Participants and spectators came and went, stopping to stroke the competing horses and chat excitedly with one another. One acre had been set up expressly for food trucks to park. The festive atmosphere was a stark contrast to the storm presently brewing between Trevor and Sabrina.

"You guys want to go grab a churro or something?" Rodrigo suggested.

Pete and Lorne hastily jumped down from the fence to join him. Once Trevor was certain the three of them were out of earshot, he rounded on Sabrina to set her straight...but she once again beat him to the punch.

"Why are you so obsessed with my ass, anyway?" She stood within inches of his face, and it would appear that *now* she had decided to lower her voice to a fierce whisper. The hot gust of her breath across his face made him shiver. It had been a week since he had gotten her alone in the barn, but the memory of her body pinned beneath his—and the sounds she had made—was never distant from his thoughts.

"You damn well know why," he growled in response. "But right now, that's beside the point. What you're wearing isn't anything like the pair of jeans you were practicing in all week. It didn't occur to you that material *that* restrictive might negatively affect our chances of winning the rescue race?"

"It seems to me like there is a lot of negativity around here—and a lot of restrictions," Sabrina noted. Her baby blue eyes flickered tellingly to his mouth. Clearly thoughts of their interlude in the stable weren't far removed from her memory, either. "Are you feeling frustrated by something, Trevor?"

Trevor didn't deign to answer that. They both knew just how frustrated he was. But there had been too much work to get done around the ranch, and their paths had rarely crossed during the day beyond the time they put aside to practice—which they were never alone for. Pete, Lorne, and Rodrigo competed here every year in calf-roping and cutting, and were ecstatic that Sabrina had been willing to foot the bill for them to put together a legitimate team. They intended to rep Wildhorse in every event and take home the prize money, along with the gaudy gold trophy—if Sabrina didn't find a way to lay her hands on it and upcycle it into something first.

But competing as a team meant very little alone time, aside from this current moment of privacy that had been granted them. Trevor didn't know which was worse at this point: no time at all with the woman who fired up his deepest desires or time only to butt heads and argue over her tight-fitting clothes.

"Kiss me," she said suddenly, and he was about to throw up his hands in defeat and sweep her into his arms when the others returned, bringing with them a bounty of churros. Sabrina turned away from Trevor to accept the offered snack with a noise of approval.

"Thanks, Rod! I haven't had one of these in forever!" she gushed, as if the only pleasure she sought in life was fair food and her prayers had been answered.

As if she *hadn't* just offered herself to him to be taken in full view of everyone.

Trevor was going to hit the roof if he didn't get away from her. He retreated to Tex's side, double- and triple-checking the saddle placement and shooting occasional glowers over the horse's back. Sabrina chatted the others up cheerfully. She was doing this on purpose, he decided, as payback for his comments on her jeans. She was making his carefully-ordered life absolutely unlivable in every aspect.

"Churro?" Several minutes later, and Sabrina was peering around underneath Tex's neck and offering him a fried-dough olive branch.

"I have no idea what the hell I'm supposed to do with you," he said.

"Oh, I'm sure you can think of a few things." She waggled her eyebrows suggestively. Tex craned his head around to investigate the churro, and she quickly held it out of reach of his horsey lips.

"You are seriously testing my focus here, Sabrina," Trevor growled. "Our event is next. In fact...."

His eyes followed Ellie Buckton, Frank's wife, as she made her way out to the center of the arena. The smattering of applause from the last event died off, and she switched her microphone on. "All right, ladies and gentlemen!" she crowed. "Next up, we have the *rescue race!*"

The audience erupted into excited cheers. Trevor watched the teasing expression on Sabrina's face sober up fast. Evidently, she hadn't noticed how many people had collected in the stands in the last five minutes. There wasn't an empty seat in the house.

"Everyone's favorite event," he supplied. He untied Tex and started to lead him toward the other assembled competitors. "Come on," he said as he mounted. "We're up third. Get up behind me and I'll ride you out to your position when the time comes."

Pete took the churro back, and Sabrina mounted, settling in behind Trevor. She wrapped her arms around his waist, and his muscles tensed reflexively. He had to focus. He couldn't let himself be distracted by all the little details of their partnership now—like the way one of her slender arms hugged him beneath the band of his belt….

The first racers were a young couple, little older than teenagers. They failed their event when the rider had to come around twice to rescue his partner, but the wide smiles on their faces as they galloped back to the start clearly showed that they were having the time of their life. The audience responded with rousing cheers once the pair had successfully crossed the finish line.

The next couple was older—likely in their thirties—and a lot more experienced. They came hurtling across the finish line in less than thirty seconds, and Ellie turned the mic back on long enough to announce that the competition's record had just been broken.

Sabrina's arms clenched nervously around his midsection. Trevor laid a pacifying hand on her elbow and squeezed.

"Here we go," he muttered below his breath. He trotted Tex out into the center of the ring.

When he felt Sabrina's hands leave his waist, he reached around to grab her arm and ease her drop to the ground. But instead of letting go, he bent low in the saddle and tugged her against the saddle.

Kissing the top of her head, he whispered against her hair. "Let's show them how good you are."

Sabrina lifted her head in surprise, the look of uncertainty on her face shifting to a smile. Giving him a brief nod, she stepped away from him to take her position waving to the crowd who cheered them on.

"That's my girl," he called out to her before turning Tex around and trotting over to the start line. He grimaced when Ellie called out that they had to beat thirty seconds.

Adjusting his stance in the saddle, he petted Tex's neck. "You ready?" The horse tossed his head in response, pawing lightly at the ground.

As the gun went off, Tex leaped forward easily reaching a gallop as they rapidly ate up the distance to Sabrina. To her credit, her stance was relaxed as she awaited their arrival.

Taking the tight turn around her, his arm was out before he thought about it and he was hoisting Sabrina onto the saddle behind him and heading back to the finish before she was fully seated. Her "oomph" followed by the tight grip of her thighs against his was all the reassurance he needed.

When they crossed the finish line, they were met with absolute silence as everyone looked to Ellie who squinted at her stop watch. Holding it up, she yelled into her microphone.

"Twenty-eight seconds!"

*   *   *

"Another round of shots!" Pete cried. He slammed his empty glass down and signaled the bartender as the bar broke into raucous laughter and cheers of approval.

"You *guys!*" Sabrina exclaimed in pleased exasperation. "You're going to drink away all our prize money before we even get home!"

Despite Sabrina's half-hearted protests, the Wildhorse team had been drinking on the house for the better part of the evening. The winning team always drank on the house at The Tin Horseshoe.

The jukebox blared, the booze flowed, and the atmosphere was charged and festive. Marcy, his ex, was trying to catch his eye from across the room, but Trevor only had eyes for one woman, and she happened to be seated right next to him.

He leaned across his stool to whisper in Sabrina's ear, "Just be glad they haven't tried drinking out of the trophy yet." The hand that wasn't holding his beer hovered over the small of her back, and Sabrina relaxed back into it. She seemed fully conscious of what she was doing, and he reveled in her own secret signals. Every glance of hers he caught seemed somehow coded; every lyric of every country song that came up on the jukebox seemed somehow written for this moment.

"I tell you!" Lorne whooped. "That's *twice* the record for the rescue race was broken in one competition! I've never seen that, not in any event in any year! Now it's the two of you who hold the record." He clinked his shot glass with Sabrina's. "And the way the boss carried you back across that finish line like that…" He cocked a sly eyebrow. "In some counties, the two of you'd be married."

Trevor recalled only too well the way their bodies had nested and rocked together as one. He eyed Sabrina sidelong, but the little blonde refused to meet his gaze. She was smiling fit to split the seams of her gorgeous face, but his intuition told him she was imagining the exact same thing. The expert way she worked her hips in the saddle…every clench and slide in perfect tandem with the way his body moved—no wonder they had won so handily. They were a good fit when it counted.

He wanted to experience that with her out of the saddle. He wanted *her,* and she knew it. She had to know it. He pressed the small of her back a little more firmly and was rewarded when her hand alighted on his knee beneath the table. He felt a stirring between his legs, but took a casual sip of his beer before entering back into the conversation.

"Sabrina's got this…this…" He gesticulated vaguely in the air above his head and chuckled. "This Christmas tree ornament she hangs above her door. Everywhere you go, ain't that right, Sabrina?"

"Yes, Trevor, that *is* right."

He was intent on driving her home tonight, so he set the beer down unfinished.

"But it's *not* a Christmas ornament," she continued for the benefit of the Wildhorse team. "It's something my grandfather gave me. I've always thought of it as a token of…good luck." She shrugged.

"I'll drink to that." Rodrigo raised his glass. "It certainly paid off for us today."

Marcy was making her way across the room now. Trevor snatched the hand in his lap and pulled Sabrina off her stool.

"Come on," he said as he dragged her out to the dance floor.

"Where are we going?" she inquired suspiciously. She tugged on their joined hands, only lightly resistant. "You're not *actually* pulling me out here to dance, are you?"

"Why wouldn't I be?" Trevor wheeled and tugged her fully into his arms. There were a few other couples out slow dancing already. He could hear the jeers coming from his employees at the bar, but knew it was only a matter time before they started clamoring to follow suit before they got left without a partner. "You're the most beautiful woman in this room," he said as they started to sway together.

"Oh, I don't know..." Sabrina blew a stray strand of hair out of her eyes and glanced up at him. "That's your ex, isn't it? The redhead over in the corner? She's pretty stunning."

"Rodrigo's already taken care of it," Trevor replied. He watched as his stable hand crossed the room to tip his hat and offer Marcy his arm. Marcy took it with a delighted smile, and they made their way out to the dance floor.

"So, is it really over between the two of you?" Sabrina asked. Trevor glanced down to take in the expression on her face. Even in the low light of the bar, her cheeks glowed warm and pink from the alcohol. She was starting to get a tan, he noticed. It only brought out those kissable freckles of hers even more.

"Yes. It's been over between us for a long time."

Sabrina gazed into his eyes. He saw a flicker of relief pass across her face. He tightened his grip on her a little more.

"While we're making confessions, there's more to that story about your grandfather's star," he mentioned. "Whatever you didn't want to say in front of the others, you can say it to me."

Sabrina turned her face away and pressed it into his shoulder. "I take that star with me everywhere," she said finally, "because of what it represents. My home burned down when I was eight years old. I remember the smoke. I remember my dad pulling my sister and me out of bed. I remember watching the fire take it all while we stood across the street. Even with such a huge fire blazing, it was so cold that night.

"We went to live with my grandparents for a bit after that. I always loved visiting them on their ranch in the summer, but try as I might, I couldn't make it feel like the extended vacation they wanted me to think of it as. So, they put me to work harder than ever, to help me take my mind off things…and they made every day more fun and challenging enough that I felt *real* satisfaction with what I had achieved. I started to look *forward* to getting up in the morning again. And by the end of it all, when we were ready to move out and start all over, Grandpa pinned that star to my chest so I would always remember what a star I was. I felt so proud. I realize how silly it sounds for a grown woman to be saying this to you," she finished abruptly.

Trevor could feel her heated cheeks through the fabric of his shirt. He was so stunned with Sabrina's story that it was several moments before he realized they had stopped dancing. He resumed with the next beat, and she followed his lead, moving with less self-assurance than she had before.

"It's not silly," he promised her. "Sometimes the people we love and the important memories tied to them imprint themselves on things. Hell, I polish my father's old rodeo saddle every morning, even though I never intend for anyone to ever use it again. It's the first thing I do when I get up, and the last thing I look at before I shut the lights off in the barn."

"I had no idea," Sabrina whispered. She looked up at him again, and this time Trevor stopped dancing deliberately. He smoothed a strand of hair back from her face and fought the inclination to lean in. He still didn't know how far she wanted to take this thing with him.

"You want to get out of here?" he asked in a throaty whisper.

Sabrina nodded. Then: "What about the horses? Don't they still need to be trailered and taken home?"

"Pete will see to it," he said. "We drew straws earlier to see who'd be in charge of the trailer."

"Very diplomatic of you, Mr. Wild," Sabrina said approvingly.

Trevor offered her his arm, and she looped her hand through it. They walked out of The Tin Horseshoe together, never pausing to look back.

Chapter 8
SABRINA

"Want me to turn the radio up?" Trevor asked her.

Sabrina nodded too quickly. "Oh…sure! I love this song!"

She grimaced in the darkness of the pickup's cab. Trevor only chuckled and reached forward to oblige her.

"It's the song we were just dancing to," he said in amusement. "'When the Stars Go Blue.'"

Why is this so awkward? Sabrina mentally berated herself. She glanced out the window but found that, for the first time ever, it was nearly impossible to pay attention to the fading sunset and vast Texas mountains. Not with Trevor sitting beside her. *Why are you so awkward? Where's the confident flirt from the rodeo earlier today? Where's the Sabrina who knows exactly how to drive Trevor Wild crazy?*

It was one thing to flirt, she realized. It was a whole other thing to know how and when to pull the trigger on these feelings both of them were fighting and failing to suppress.

What would be so wrong about giving over to her attraction, anyway? She could practically hear her manager, Stacy, on the phone now: *Sabrina, the way you have conducted yourself in this instance is utterly unprofessional and will forever be whispered of around the office as 'the Wildhorse Incident.' Your picture and resume will be framed in the hallway as an example of how* not *to conduct yourself with a client, ever. You're fired, and also, I never liked you in the first place.*

Okay, so maybe she knew for a fact that Stacy liked her and that no catastrophe on *that* massive a scale was bound to happen if she succumbed. Still, there was something stopping her from reaching out and taking that chance with Trevor.

And with the cowboy now sitting in silence beside her, she wasn't sure he was ready to take the risk, either. Trevor was methodical; he was set in his ways. He had already changed so much of his life just to allow her to jam her foot through the door. Was it fair to expect anything more from him? Was it possible— *really* possible—that the strength of her attraction to him could be reciprocated?

"Where are we?" Sabrina asked suddenly. They were driving up an unfamiliar hill that overlooked Wildhorse Ranch. She rolled her window down and poked her head out in wonder. The sun was down now, and the stars...the stars were *incredible,* scattered white gemstones across the navy blue night sky. It was all she could do to keep herself from gasping audibly at the sight overhead.

"Come on." Trevor put the truck in park and got out of the car. Sabrina followed suit and joined him around back. He unlatched and opened up the bed, before holding his hand out to her to help her step up.

"You keep a bedroll back here?" she asked suspiciously. The truck bed rocked as Trevor pulled himself up after her.

"Sure. I keep most of my camping stuff back here." He untied and unfurled the bedroll. It was incredible to Sabrina that such a simple gesture could make her feel more like royalty than she ever had before in her life. She moved onto the mat and laid back. Trevor aligned himself beside her.

"So you're telling me you bring girls out here all the time," she teased.

"Never brought a soul out here with me," Trevor promised. He turned his head toward her. "But after your story about that star, and how much it means to you, I thought I'd like to give you a star to hold onto as well. You can choose whichever one you want." He pointed up toward the night sky. Without the light pollution of the city, Sabrina could clearly see the brilliant, beautiful smear of the Milky Way.

There was nothing she could say in response to Trevor's gesture. Nothing she could do, except turn into him and press her lips against his.

He held himself still beside her. When she deepened the kiss, and even made to slide up against his chest, he took hold of her shoulders and pushed her onto her back. The rich taste of the beer he had been drinking lingered on his tongue, but Trevor wasn't anywhere close to being drunk—he would have never agreed to drive her home if he wasn't in his right mind.

They had expended all their words for the evening. Every argument, every clever quip and talking point, faded from existence as Trevor Wild took her in his arms and kissed her until the stars spun overhead. His hand slid up her stomach to grip her breast, and Sabrina aided him by stripping her shirt off and throwing it into the far corner of the truck.

A gust of cold night air, combined with Trevor's forceful fingers, coaxed her nipples to tautness. Sabrina let her head fall back. She tried to even out her breathing, but her efforts proved fruitless the moment Trevor lowered his mouth to take her other breast into the warmth of his mouth.

"Ah!" Sabrina gasped and strained against him, but there was no resistance to be mounted against such a wonderful sensation. His tongue traced the tight flesh; his teeth teasing her. She thought she would go mad, so riled and so unfulfilled. Her hands found the front of his jeans and jerked them open. He groaned a light "careful" below his breath, but never ceased in his attentions.

Before she could get his pants down and take the erection she could see straining against his boxers into her hands, Trevor drew back from her. Sabrina made a throaty noise of dismay, but he had only withdrawn to help her wriggle out of her jeans. Despite what he might have thought about their restrictiveness, they slid off her easily now, exposing her hot pink thong. She heard him groan again as he fell upon her. *Trevor likes thongs,* she realized with a wicked smile. It was certainly an observation she intended to file away for later, but soon enough he was groping and kissing and thrusting himself against her fit to make her senseless.

"The back pocket of my jeans," she gasped. She turned her eyes from him only for a moment to hunt the shadows of the truck, but she couldn't see where all her discarded clothes had gone. "I have—"

"I've got us covered," Trevor groaned into the hollow of her throat. "My wallet."

A new sensation came over her as she slid a hand into his back pocket and located the square of old, worn leather. His quiet reassurance deepened the flush, the warmth, of the arousal that spread through her.

I've got us covered.

Sabrina drew his wallet out and extracted the condom. "I've got *you* covered," she whispered. She made eye contact as she tore the plastic packaging open with her teeth; Trevor groaned.

She worked the condom down over his erection slowly, relishing the easy way her hands slid over the latex. The additional lubrication it provided was heavenly—she could only imagine how it felt for Trevor.

Apparently, the teasing stroke of her hands proved increasingly unbearable. As much as he might have approved of her choice in underwear, it was off in the next instant, and Trevor flung it into the corner of the truck bed. He shucked his own even faster.

When he eased himself into her slick, tight passage for the first time, Sabrina arched herself off the bedroll and whimpered. Trevor was massive but it wasn't enough—it wasn't nearly enough. Only when he started to rock against her did she get a fleeting glimpse of how she might be satisfied. She was desperate—desperate for pressure, desperate for friction, desperate for Trevor to lose himself in her the same way she was losing herself in him.

"Trevor...yes..." she begged him in whispers. "I've wanted this for so long. *Please.*" She didn't even care if she was making sense. Her body spoke to him louder than her words, and Trevor knew exactly what she wanted. He increased his pace, thrusting and lunging into her. Sabrina bucked and cried beneath him, and he slipped his arms beneath the bend in her back to clutch her to him.

"Sabrina." The way he groaned her name made her shudder. She cupped his face in her hands, relishing how the tension in his jaw matched the clenched, unbearable tension of her body. Every hitch in his hip movements against her own, every new take on the rhythm they made together, heated the coil of pleasure inside her. Every deep, penetrative plunge of his rigid length threatened to overwhelm her anew with its girth; she could scarcely believe there was room enough inside her.

It was a ride she certainly had no intention of being rescued from.

"Trevor," she murmured again. There was something more lingering on the tip of her tongue than just the too-fleeting taste of him. His kisses were an addiction she couldn't satisfy no matter how much she tilted her chin and begged breathlessly for them. His tongue seemed to harden in tandem with every thrust of his cock, until she had trouble keeping track of where and when he invaded her. He filled her utterly—mind, body, and soul. If only she could find the words to convey to him just how *much* she needed him.

The heat of his chest and the delicious sensation of being overfull with him made her peak too soon. Sabrina tried desperately to resist the pressure building inside her, but there was no hope for it—and if there ever had been, Trevor's uttered oath would have put her over anyway.

"Oh, *fuck.*"

Her hips collided with his rough downward thrust as his body jerked against hers. She opened her mouth to cry out, and Trevor took her cry into him in a single, earth-shattering kiss.

Sabrina collapsed into his arms, and Trevor pulled his work coat over them to keep the cold off. Sabrina snuggled close to his chest, and felt herself starting to drowse as his thundering heartbeat slowed and lulled her into complete complacency. The stars winked overhead, a silent, approving party to their union.

"We'd better get back," Trevor said eventually. Sabrina turned in his arms, smiled dreamily, and nodded. The night around them was chilly, but she didn't intend to be out of his embrace for long.

But the road to the overlook wasn't the only unexpected turn Trevor took that night. Sabrina paused in unclipping her seatbelt when she realized that they hadn't gone back to her bunkhouse, or even to the main house. Trevor pulled up to the barn and killed the engine.

Then—without any trace of irony or hint that he was pulling her leg—he pulled one of his checklists out of his back pocket.

"I've got a few things to take care of," he muttered. "And as soon as the horses get back, I'm going to wrap Tex's legs and make sure he's plenty hydrated after that run."

"Oh...right." Sabrina sat back in her seat and stared incredulously out the window. What could she say to that? She wasn't hard-hearted enough to suggest that Trevor should forget his horses for the evening and focus solely on *her*. Still...she had hoped that...

"Okay. Just promise me you'll get to bed at a reasonable hour, all right? Goodnight." She turned quickly away from him so he wouldn't be able to see the expression on her face.

"Sabrina—" he began.

But she had already let herself down out of the truck. She shut the door behind her and flipped him a wave, grinning from ear to ear. She then turned and started across the lawn for the bunkhouse.

Alone.

Chapter 9
TREVOR

"You're mad at me," Trevor stated. "You can go ahead and admit it."

He had roped Sabrina into helping him clear out the attic of the farmhouse. He had been so busy enjoying the view of her doubled over and crawling between boxes, her tight posterior clad in those ridiculous jeans, that he almost hadn't noticed the other, more dangerous current in the air.

"I'm not mad," she stated. Her perfect teeth clipped together audibly at the end of her assertion.

"Uh-huh." Trevor kept his eyes on her. He didn't believe a word of it.

"It's just that..." she continued in exasperation. He sat back and drew his knee up to his chest as he waited for the truth to come pouring out of her, and Sabrina didn't disappoint. She turned and exhaled enormously. "It's just that I didn't want the other night to end the way it did. It was *so* perfect—maybe the most perfect day I've ever had in my life—and then you...then..."

Her comments surprised the hell out of him. Trevor wanted to protest, but he still had no idea why she was angry with him. All he could do was wait for her to get the words out.

Sabrina slapped her knees and scooted closer to him. "Seriously, Trevor?" she demanded. "You have no idea *why* I might be a little pissed off right now? I wanted to grab another beer with you. I wanted to invite you back to my cabin and spend the *night* with you, and you just…you just…."

"Got called away to work." He hadn't thought of it from Sabrina's perspective. He had thought about going back to her bunkhouse with her, sure, but when the invitation hadn't come, he had shrugged it off as her not wanting anyone on the staff to see him leaving in the morning or—as had happened before—her wanting some space after the most recent shift in their relationship.

Sabrina sighed so roughly it was a growl. "You didn't *have* to work right there and then, Trevor."

Trevor's brows together. He didn't like feeling stupid. Marcy had accused him of being a lug more than once, but he had never been able to read the women in his life as well as he read horses.

"I didn't realize," he admitted finally. "I thought…I thought you needed more space to think about things. About us."

Sabrina fiddled with her earring and stared at the dusty wood floor beneath them. Finally, she pointed to something behind him. "I'll forgive you," she said, *"if* you give me that bowl. That one. There."

Trevor craned around to look. He had just been building a pile of items to discard. At the top of the pile was an old copper bowl that had belonged to his grandmother.

"What do you want that for?" he asked her. No matter how he tried to imagine a use for it, he just couldn't.

Sabrina moved in close beside him and pulled the bowl into her lap. "I'm going to use it to make something beautiful," she promised.

He watched the way she lovingly stroked the bowl in her hand. His grandmother, he decided in that moment, would have loved Sabrina.

"Trust me," she persisted. "This is going to be put to good use. But I'd like it to be a surprise, if that's okay."

Trevor's mouth twitched itself into a smile. "Normally I don't like surprises," he reminded her. Sabrina just leaned in and pressed a swift kiss to his cheek. She pulled back with a satisfied giggle—one that soon resolved itself into surprised, full-throated laughter as Trevor pushed the bowl out of her lap and pinned her to the floor beneath him.

"What, right *here?*" she gasped as he ravished her neck. "Mr. Wild, I didn't think you liked surprises!"

"I know what I like," he reassured. "I also know where and when I like it."

"Mmm," Sabrina hummed in approval as he began to unbutton the front of her blouse. "Are you sure? You might not be able to strike 'clean attic' off your checklist for the day."

"Screw the checklist," Trevor growled.

"Now *that* is certainly a surprise!" Sabrina laughed with delight as he lowered himself to her once more. Having her here with him, beneath him, made it remarkably easy to savor the snatched unexpectedness of the moment—and to forget about his work obligations. There were chores that needed to be seen to, certainly, but they would still be waiting for him when he caught hold of himself again.

Right now, it was Sabrina that had captivated him. He paused, lips hovering above her skin, with only room left between them to breathe. He took his time slowly inhaling the familiar floral scent of her hair; when he pressed his mouth to the tender spot just below her ear, he tasted the clean comfort of her. He lost himself in listening to the faint, ecstatic throb of her pulse, before the sound of his own heart beating in his ears overwhelmed it.

He spoke before he realized his brain had given his mouth orders to do so.

"Sabrina, this thing between us...."

She stilled beneath him, but it wasn't resistance. He drew back to look at her. Her blonde hair fanned out around her pale, beautiful face like fire wreaths the sun. The flush in her cheeks brought out every freckle. Her eyes had freckles, too, he realized, flecks and flares of emerald green, lost but not beyond discovery in the blues of her irises.

"We don't have to put a name to it," she breathed. "Not if you don't want to."

Something in her face told him otherwise. She looked so vulnerable laid beneath him...yet the softness of her face was less pronounced all of a sudden. There was more steel there than he remembered. Was she guarding herself—protecting herself—from the noncommittal answer she claimed to have no stake in?

He couldn't guess what answer was the right one; all he could do was give her the true one.

"I think I'm falling in love with you, Sabrina Hearthstone."

In all his past relationships, he had never been the first to say it—now, he wasn't sure he had ever really meant it, or known what it was he was confessing. Not like this.

Sabrina's eyelashes fluttered, like butterflies taken by a surprise gust of wind. "I think I'm falling for you too, Trevor Wild," she whispered. She raised herself up on one elbow, cupped his face, and pressed her lips to his. The lightness of the touch, combined with their words, made his heart stutter to an almost-stop in his chest.

His hands slid down her body, reverent in their exploration. He took this new knowledge of what she felt for him and relearned everything he knew about her: her trim waist, her taut abdomen, the dimple of her belly button and the smooth, velvet plane leading to heaven below. He laid his lips upon her stomach as his finger caught in the front of her pants and inched them down her hips. He could have sworn he heard Sabrina purr.

"Mmm." Her suppressed moan was delicious, and with every inch of her that was revealed he pressed a subsequent kiss to her skin. She arched her hips off the ground as he tugged her jeans, her underwear, all the way down her slender legs. She kicked them away as he dragged his lips along her inner thigh. *"Trevor."* The way she hissed his name as he savored her was sweet, sensual music to his ears.

His kisses carried him back up between Sabrina's legs, and he darted his tongue out to taste her wet, pink center. God, there was nothing better than listening to the way her breath hitched and her hips bucked hard into the floor when he did that. He licked and sucked and nibbled her until her thighs quaked on either side of his head; then he grasped her legs and continued a minute more for good measure.

"Oh, God," she moaned. "You're good at everything. It's not fair."

"Are you about to come already?" he murmured, lifting his eyes from between her legs to look at her. Judging by the wanton way she had her own eyes fixed upon him and the way she gasped and panted, he thought he had his answer. Before she could claim something contrary, he grabbed her hips and pulled her upright with him. He crossed his legs beneath them and settled her onto his lap.

The next few seconds were a blur as Sabrina fought his fervent, unrelenting kisses, laughing as she struggled to get her hands between them. His belt slithered free, and she practically ripped the front of his jeans open, aided by the fact that he was already straining to be free of them anyway. She encased his erection in her fist, and Trevor's breath caught at the firm pressure.

"You *really* want this," he noted as he yanked his shirt up over his head.

"I'm not the one so obviously bursting at the seams for it," Sabrina retorted. As soon as he had dispensed with his T-shirt, Trevor snatched her face in his hands and thrust his tongue into her gasping mouth—just to show her there were better things to do in that instant than sass him. Sabrina pushed into him eagerly, releasing his cock only long enough to shed her own shirt. Her bare skin felt on fire against his.

Trevor dropped his hands, grasping either side of her ass as he pulled her in closer. Her legs clenched around his waist as he raised then lowered her onto his rigid cock. Sabrina, already slick between the legs from his earlier attentions, undulated her hips just once, and he slid inside her without resistance.

A shared, explosive groan rocked them both. Trevor buried his face in her shoulder as Sabrina threw her head back, but his body wouldn't let him pause to catch his breath now. He jounced Sabrina in his lap; his fingers grasped and worked her waist as she rode him. The sensation of her breasts pressed hard against his chest drove him wild. She took over the rhythm, and his hands slid up the small of her back, skimming beads of perspiration as they went.

"You're so goddamned beautiful," he whispered. A tangled, sweat-soaked lock of hair fell across her face as she glanced down at him, her cries mounting. She was beyond response, but she had heard him. That was all that mattered.

Trevor tensed beneath her, but Sabrina's hips kept their course, circling and stirring him around inside her. His abdominals tightened, and heat flooded him in a rush; he banded his arms around her back and held her close as he shuddered to completion. His hips gave a few more questing thrusts, and Sabrina's voice broke on a cry of ecstasy. Her slight frame trembled in his arms as an orgasm took her, and Trevor groaned at the beautiful sight. He carried her down with him, kissing her fervently and relishing the astonished, bell-like clarity of her laugh.

"Still think I'm good at everything?" he asked in a spent whisper. He pushed a lock of hair out of her eyes as she smiled sleepily at him.

"Good at everything," she repeated, "but *great* at one thing in particular. Feel free to check 'getting laid' off your list for the day."

It wasn't on his list for the day. *But,* Trevor reflected, *I wouldn't mind making it a recurring item.*

*   *   *

"Boss!"

Pete was shouting and running down the driveway waving his arms. Trevor raised himself off his outside work bench in alarm. Pete was his most laid-back ranch hand—any show of panic from him meant that either something vital was on fire, or it was about to be.

"Sabrina sent me to get you!" Pete pulled his hat off and pointed off toward the bunkhouses. "You better come quick!"

Trevor dropped the tack he was cleaning. He didn't ask questions or demand elaboration; he heard Sabrina's name and came, leaving his own hat and gloves behind him and throwing up clouds of dirt as he sprinted ahead of Pete. "She's in the west bunkhouse!" Pete called after him.

It should have struck him as suspicious that his ranch hand didn't follow.

When he got to the bunkhouse, he mounted the steps in a single leap and threw the door open. "Sabrina?" he hollered into the house. He didn't smell fire, didn't see smoke, didn't hear screaming, only—

"D-don't come in here!" Sabrina called back to him. Her muffled voice came from the direction of the bathroom; what's more, it sounded panicked. Trevor strode across the length of the front room. He stopped only when his boot *sloshed* into the carpet.

He stared down in horror. Half of the living room was soggy with water.

Sabrina.

He didn't say the culprit's name out loud. He couldn't. He didn't want to wrap his head around the fact that the woman he...the woman...that Sabrina could cause *this* much damage.

Trevor completed his line to the bathroom and threw the door open. Sabrina glanced up from where she crouched beneath the sink. She was completely drenched from head to toe; her blonde hair was dark with saturation, and her white shirt was plastered to her chest. A memory flashed across Trevor's mind, and he recalled the time she had accidentally sprayed herself down with the hose.

But this...this was much, much worse. The bathroom was in absolute chaos. The shower curtain rod was pulled down, and water was gushing out of the cabinet Sabrina knelt partway inside. Even from here he could see that she had tried—and failed—to staunch the flow of water with her shirt.

"I...I was just trying to install the new basin," she stammered. "I had the YouTube video keyed up and everything." She gestured to her laptop, which was perched precariously on the back of the toilet.

"Jesus," Trevor cursed. "Hand that thing to me and let me put it in the kitchen before it shorts."

Sabrina complied, and he had the short walk to the kitchen and back to master his temper and think of what to say to her.

When he returned, he exploded.

Chapter 10
Sabrina

"Where the hell am I supposed to find the extra couple thousand dollars to fix this?" Trevor bellowed.

Tears stung the corners of Sabrina's eyes. She thought she had seen Trevor lose his temper plenty of times before on account of her; now, she could see how awfully mistaken she had been. Even when she had done something to frustrate him in the past, he had never raised his voice to anything resembling this decibel level. For the first time since meeting him, she saw the man that everyone else in Lockhart Bend found so formidable.

"Calm down, Trevor. I'm…it was an accident!" she exclaimed. "This should be an easy enough thing to fix, if you'll let me—"

"Where am I supposed to come up with the money, Sabrina?" he shouted. "Sell a horse? Because that's what it's going to take—you know that, right?"

"Apparently I don't know anything," she whispered dangerously. "So why don't you go ahead and tell me?"

Trevor was so angry his hands shook. He pointed a finger at her, just to give it something to do, a task to complete. "I can't afford to part with a horse right now, Sabrina. Not a single one.

The bank payment on the ranch is due tomorrow. *Tomorrow.* There's no money left to fix this."

She could fix this. She knew she could, if only he'd give her a chance. She tried to fold her hands over his finger in a mollifying gesture, but Trevor yanked his hand back as if her touch burned. Anxiety radiated off him more powerfully than his anger, and she realized the depths of what her attempts to remodel had just cost him.

Trevor ran a desperate hand over his close-cropped hair and exhaled deeply through his nose. "I'm not sure how this is supposed to work."

He appeared to be muttering to himself, but Sabrina heard his words loud and clear. Sharp as any knife, they cut to the heart of her. She felt as if she had been unceremoniously drenched by another round of freezing cold water.

There was no way to come back from this. This was the straw that had broken the cowboy's back. All those times she had tried and failed and thought that Trevor had forgiven her…she could see now that he had been building a mental checklist of her shortcomings. Even she had to admit to herself that when the pros and cons of keeping her here were weighed, she continued to tip the scales in her own disfavor.

If Trevor decided to postpone the glamping program, it was likely Sabrina would lose her job. She wouldn't ask Trevor to lie for her and tell her boss *she* wasn't the problem. She would lose her job, and someone else would come in and finish the setup for her.

But she wasn't concerned about her job right now. First and foremost, all Sabrina wanted to do in that instant was throw her arms around him. She wanted to tell him how sorry she was. Instead, the two of them stood in silence watching the water continue to trickle out of the busted hole in the wall.

When she finally departed, she didn't think he noticed. Maybe it was better that way. She kept the memory of his bowed back with her as she crossed the lawn and locked herself inside her cabin. She thought about the anger, the disappointment, in his flaming black eyes, and she buried her face in her pillow and sobbed until her down feathers were drowning.

She rose hours later to take her ruined makeup off and wash her face. She put a pot of coffee on and slumped over the bar at the kitchen.

Her grandfather's star glinted over the cabin's doorway, but even that couldn't bring her any comfort tonight.

She would make everything right. In the morning—she would make everything right.

* * *

Sabrina hadn't expected a long wait at the Lockhart Bend Pawn Shop. *He's doing a booming business,* she thought as she studied the smiling, jovial broker behind the desk. *And he's sure taking his sweet time.*

She tweaked her sunglasses down her nose a little to take in her surroundings. She liked to think she was incognito, but she probably wasn't fooling anybody who cared to look. She could already imagine the small-town gossip that might accompany sighting Wildhorse's glamping coordinator at a pawn shop. Then again, maybe she was being paranoid.

The shop was large, but appeared smaller for its stacked shelves and controlled clutter. The atmosphere was surprisingly less morose than she had expected. Her neighbors sipped their take-out coffees and chatted with one another about the weather, their children's sporting events, and other minutia of everyday life.

She wondered how many of the people standing in line in front of her were there because of one massive mistake.

It was hard to keep what had happened with Trevor in perspective. On the one hand, she had tried her hardest and only ever operated with the best intentions. On the other, it seemed like everything she had attempted since arriving at the ranch had completely blown up in her face. She was a *good* adventure coordinator, maybe even a great one—but that didn't change the fact that almost nothing had gone right since her arrival here.

She would make it right. But once she had done that, what came next for her? She couldn't ask Trevor to keep her on after so many screw-ups. No way. *Maybe* she could find another ranch near the retirement home and stay near her grandparents, but again, Sabrina knew what the gossip was bound to be like. How many places would be willing to give her a chance after her complete and utter failure at Wildhorse?

And what about her budding romance with Trevor? Somehow, the master upcycler in her couldn't imagine a world where she was able to salvage *that*. Maybe it was better to leave things like they had, cold and cordial-like, and pack her things and go. She didn't fit into his carefully-ordered world, and he…

Sabrina shoved her sunglasses back up her nose. She had already cried more in the past twenty-four hours than she had when her parents' house burned down. Tears were one detail she could hide from any gossip-mongers.

The person in front of her concluded his business and moved aside. She was up. She stepped to the desk and was reaching into her bag when the bell over the shop's door jingled. She turned in faint curiosity to see who else had business there, considering it felt as if the entire town was in attendance already, and blanched at who she saw. Her heart leapt into her throat in the same instant Trevor laid eyes on her and froze in the doorway.

Once the initial shock had passed, she dropped her eyes to what he was carrying with him. His arms were loaded down with a gorgeous, chestnut-brown saddle. *Not just any saddle,* Sabrina realized. *His father's rodeo saddle.*

What the hell was he doing *here* with *that?*

Their shock at seeing one another had made them conspicuous to the other customers. It was as if the entire pawn shop had stopped to hold its breath. Finally, Trevor broke the silence. "Sabrina, can I talk to you outside?"

"Want to leave that here with me?" the pawnshop owner asked her. He gestured to the small cloth-wrapped item in her hand. "I can appraise it for you while you're out."

Sabrina glanced from the owner to Trevor and back again. "Um…give me one second." She hustled out the door after Trevor.

His pickup was parked at the curb. He tossed the saddle down into the open bed, took a deep breath, and turned back to her. "What are you doing here?" he finally asked. He folded his arms expectantly when she didn't answer him. "I saw you left early this morning. I guess I just assumed…."

He trailed off, and they both stood in uncomfortable silence. Sabrina realized he had thought *exactly* what she had been planning a half-second ago: that she had left the ranch for good without a word of goodbye.

"I'm…" She steeled herself to continue before raising her chin defiantly. With her shades fixed over her eyes, there was no way he could see what she was really thinking in that moment. "I'm here to get the money I owe you. The money for repairs to the bunkhouse bathroom." She was proud of the way her voice didn't shake in the slightest.

"With what?" he asked her pointedly. His eyes fell to the palm-sized, folded cloth in her hand. She would have liked to have kept him guessing, but his eyebrows shot up instantly, and he snatched her hand in his. "Are you crazy? Absolutely not! There is no way you're selling your grandfather's star. Besides, it's not worth—"

"Listen!" Sabrina jerked her hand back quickly. "I know what I'm doing, Trevor. I know it's my grandfather's star, but I don't need that broker to appraise it for me. I had it appraised a long time ago. I always thought it was a lot heavier than it looked." She paused, drew a deep breath, and continued. "It's made out of gold. My grandfather just painted it over with silver so it would look more like an Old West sheriff's star when I was a kid. It's worth more than it looks at first glance."

"That star is priceless to *you*," Trevor whispered.

Sabrina's lip quivered. Why was he being so nice to her? Didn't he see she was trying to do the right thing by him? "It's a trinket," she said. "Having it with me has gotten me through a lot, but maybe I don't need it like I think I do. Even though I…I know I have to leave Wildhorse." She drew in another quick breath. "I *know* that. But I guess a part of me wished that…if I brought you the money and asked you for forgiveness…you'd let me stay." She waved the ornament in the air. "And I wouldn't have to keep hanging this damn star over every new door of every new place that I lived. It's worth it, Trevor. Even if you don't want me to stay, let me do this."

"Sabrina, I want you to stay," he said firmly.

Sabrina blinked. Wondering if he was taking one last opportunity to mess with her, she stared hard up into his grim face, but she couldn't see that he was getting any sort of sick, vengeful pleasure out of this exchange.

"I…" She broke off and wheeled to wave *both* hands at the back of his truck. "What are *you* doing down here, anyway? What is this? Why do you have your father's saddle with you? You weren't actually thinking about *pawning* it to cover the repairs that were my fault to begin with, were you?"

Trevor rubbed the stubble of his jaw. He shifted uncomfortably in front of her, and appeared to be weighing his words. Finally, he spoke:

"I'm not gonna deny that what you said to me touches me," he said. "And…and that what you said just now ring true. I feel the exact same way you do, Sabrina." He gestured to the saddle. "I want to make a change. And maybe that change comes with letting go of something that I've thought valuable for all these years. The future—and a possible future with *you*—is more precious than any relic from my past."

Sabrina felt a tear slip down her cheek. So much for hiding. Trevor's grimace softened, and he stepped to her to remove her sunglasses.

"Let me do this," he whispered. "Let me be the hero who lets you keep your grandfather's star. Let me be the man who admits that maybe, all this time, he's been doing things wrong." He smoothed the pad of his thumb across her cheek and banished the tears. "Please don't let me be the man who loses the one thing that matters most to him."

Despite his efforts to skim her tears away, his words opened the floodgates. Sabrina gasped in relief and threw her arms around him. He caught and steadied her, like she knew he would. Cupping the back of her head, she felt his chest shake in a relieved chuckle.

"Sabrina, I *love* that you would give up something so precious for me," he whispered. His lips drifted along her hairline, and he cemented a kiss to her temple. "But what I love more is you and seeing you happy."

"I love you too," she managed to choke out. Of all the places she had dreamed of confessing the depths of her feelings for Trevor Wild, she had never imagined it would be in front of a pawn shop—but in that moment, she couldn't bring herself to care about the circumstances. The home, the *man,* she had longed for, were hers.

She clung to him as long as he allowed. When he eventually gave a polite cough, she drew back and wiped her eyes roughly. Trevor's handsome face flexed in a smile, and his dark gaze fixed her with such affection that it left Sabrina feeling winded. She sat down in the open bed of the truck beside the saddle. In the next instant, she was reaching to stall Trevor as he wrapped his arms around the saddle, but he shrugged her off gently and hauled it up against his chest.

"Let me do this, Sabrina," he murmured. "Then let me take you down the street and buy you a coffee."

"All right," she conceded. She watched him disappear inside the pawn shop. Moments later, he came back out with a substantive wad of cash. He stowed it in his wallet and presented her with the gravest thumbs-up she had ever seen. Sabrina gave a short laugh despite herself and wiped her eyes again for good measure. She let her rescue rider lift her down off the back of the truck and kiss her.

"Can I ask one thing from you?" he inquired as he pulled away. She nodded. *Anything,* she thought as she gazed up at him in adoration. "I want to hang that star of yours off the rearview mirror of the pickup," he said. He walked around to the passenger side of his truck and pulled open the door for her. "Think that's something we can agree on?"

"Agreed," she said as she climbed in.

"How'd you get down here, anyway?" Trevor asked as he folded himself behind the wheel. "Pete's truck was still in the driveway when I left."

"Uber," Sabrina said. His dark brows drew together, and she gesticulated to her smartphone. "Lockhart Bend has all of *one* driver in operation. Guess I got lucky."

"I don't know what the hell that is," Trevor replied. Sabrina glanced at him sharply to see if he was joking, but his stone-faced demeanor betrayed nothing. He put the truck in reverse and angled them back out into the road.

"I'm going to pretend you didn't just say that," she replied. "Otherwise I might have to rethink falling for such a stubborn, backwoods, averse-to-change hunk in a—"

But the very cowboy hat that she had been about to deride came off that very same instant, and Trevor swooped in to capture her smart mouth in his. Sabrina gave a half-muffled laugh of delight and grabbed hold of his square, rough face to keep him from retreating. Not even the changing stoplight could stop his surprising show of affection, and Sabrina… thanked her lucky star that she had finally found a home to call her own.

CHAPTER 11
TREVOR

Trevor stared across the ring watching as the Glamper guests stared enthralled at Pete working with Tex. While Pete was a slow talker, his speech had become exaggerated as the guests seemed to glom onto his every word.

"Now, don't you mind Tex here none, he can be downright frisky if you give him too much rein...."

Pete's voice blurred as he felt someone walk up to join him. Thinking it was Sabrina, he turned to her with a smile only to have it freeze on his face.

"Marcy." He tipped his hat to her before turning back to concentrate on Pete.

"You've been avoiding me, Trevor," she told him as she rested one foot on the fence in front of them. "If I didn't know better, I might think you didn't want to speak to me."

Sighing loudly, he slapped his work gloves against his jeans. "You're right. I have. Nothing much to say."

Nodding her head, she also watched Pete, not saying anything. They both turned their heads when they heard Sabrina's cheerful voice directing the guests toward the next activity as they all excitedly followed her.

"I think you're missing out on arts and crafts or something. I heard she has two bedazzlers."

Marcy's loud laugh broke the ice that had grown between them. Reaching out, she squeezed his arm before turning to walk away. Stopping, she turned back around.

"You did good here."

Tipping his head, he agreed with her. "I did."

"And Sabrina? She seems nice."

"She is."

"Maybe a bit…spontaneous."

Trevor couldn't hide the grimace. "That she is."

Marcy laughed again. "It's good to see you're finally stepping out of that rigid box you put yourself in. You're doing a good thing, Trevor. Don't be a stranger, okay?"

She didn't wait for his answer as she turned and followed the others to the barn.

"Was that Marcy?" a voice said from behind him. Looking over his shoulder, he adjusted his hat as his brother joined him. "What's she doing here?"

"She's here for the glamper experience," he said, tapping his gloves on his jeans.

"Damn, okay. And what does Sabrina think about it?" Trent asked him.

Trevor shrugged. "She hasn't said anything or been acting any different, so I guess things are okay."

"You guess...."

"You here for anything special, Sheriff Wild?" Trevor was not in the mood to talk about his current girlfriend or his ex with his brother.

"You heard from Charlie or Pam lately?"

"Not since the holidays. Why, what's going on? Is everything okay?" While Trevor wasn't that close to his half-brother, he still tried to keep up with how he was doing but lately, he'd been so busy.

"He's been injured. Torn ACL or something. Looks like our little brother might be coming home for a bit while he recuperates," Trent told him.

"Oh damn." Before Trevor could say anything else, Trent's radio crackled. Turning, he stepped away to answer the call.

"I gotta go. Problem in town. I'll let you know what I find out."

"Thanks. I'd appreciate that and I'll try calling Pam."

"You do that." As Trent walked back toward his car, he called out. "You done good here. Granddad would be proud."

Trevor wasn't sure what to say, so he raised his hand in acknowledgement. That was the second person to say that.

Walking toward the barn, he peeked in on the guests who were happily mucking out stalls and laying out fresh straw for the horses.

He was about to comment that this wasn't on the list of approved activities when he felt Sabrina's hand on his waist. Wrapping his arm around her shoulders, he pulled her tight against him.

"What's all this?" he asked her.

"Maybe you should talk to Pete about that. He was commenting about how much work he still had to do today and how much he wished he had more time to spend with the guests. They immediately volunteered to help him with his chores. That man is a master manipulator. I think I need to take lessons," Sabrina told him as she laughed. "I swear he has them wrapped around his little finger. Even Marcy agreed to help and she should know better."

Trevor coughed out a laugh as some of the guests turned to look at them. Tipping his hat, he tugged Sabrina into one of the clean stalls and shut the door.

"Trevor, what are you doing?" she hissed. "Not in front of the guests."

"What? Can't a man spend a bit of time with his favorite filly?" he teased.

"Oh, you so did not just compare me to a horse," she whispered back.

The look of shock and anger on her face was too much and his face broke out in a wide grin. Pulling his hat off, he tossed it on a hay bale before pulling her close.

Wrapping his arms around her, he kissed the top of her head before tilting her chin up to kiss her lightly.

"You are doing a fantastic job and I can't thank you enough. Because of you, Wildhorse Ranch will flourish."

Sabrina opened and closed her mouth, unsure what to say and only stopped when he kissed her. When they surfaced for air, she pushed back from his chest.

"I should go see how the guests are doing before Pete has them fixing fences," she told him. As she opened the door, she stopped. "You really think so?"

"I do."

He could see the look of pride come across her face.

"You know, you're a very lucky man."

Trevor knew why he was lucky but he was curious what she thought. "Oh, how's that?"

"You have an awesome girlfriend who loves you." Walking through the door, she called down to the guests. "Who wants to bedazzle a horseshoe?" she called out.

Laughing, Trevor reached to pick up his hat and set it back on his head. "Yep. I am a very lucky man."

Epilogue
TREVOR

Trevor paused in his work to wipe the sweat from his brow.

He could afford to take a break from his chores, he decided. The old barn wasn't going to clean itself, but he needed to refuel. He pulled his gloves off and crossed to the old coffee maker he had unearthed earlier. A few rinses with hot water and soap, and he had felt adventurous enough to actually try and use it out there in the barn, and he was not disappointed. It worked like a charm, and he wondered idly what Sabrina would have to say about his salvaging it when she returned from town.

Trevor poured himself a refill of the robust black brew, stirred in a sugar cube for the hell of it, and leaned against the barn door with a sigh of contentment. Only when he was alone like this could he truly take it all in. He watched the white morning mist receding slowly from the pastures, watched the horses grazing quietly on the dew-freshened grass.

He saw the cloud of dirt billowing up from the road before he saw the ranch's pickup. He watched as Sabrina made the turn into Wildhorse and slowed as she came up on the barn. She hung out the window, grinning from ear-to-ear.

"Morning, cowboy!" she shouted.

Trevor detached from the doorway to come out and meet her, his own smile tucking up one corner of his face. "You're gettin' real handy with driving that thing." He nodded toward the truck. Sabrina leaned out further, looking radiant enough to outshine the Texas sun, and the rancher bent to press a welcoming kiss to her lips.

"Don't be mad," she preempted as he drew away. Trevor raised an eyebrow in amusement.

"Mrs. Miller treat you okay?"

Grimacing. "No, she's still mad about the beds. Ever since Mr. Miller found out how much I was willing to pay for them, he's been doing his best to sell off as much as he can to me at a tidy profit. I think they both still see me as some sort of city girl who doesn't know a copper bowl from a tin box. Thankfully, I have a trick or two up my sleeve and I'm still getting good deals from them."

"Well you're doing everyone a good service even getting the Millers to let you on the property let alone buy anything. I still can't believe you talked her out of pressing charges."

"I know. Mrs. Miller went out and bought a new padlock for one of the barns and won't give her husband the key. I'm dying to find out what she has hidden in there," she said with a laugh.

Sabrina popped open the door and stepped down from the cab. "What have you been working on all morning? You never told me *why* you were clearing out this old barn. You know our next batch of glampers is scheduled to show up tomorrow, and you're bound to get one or two of them walking through here by accident. What's the big secret?"

"Come and see." Trevor wrapped his arm around her slender shoulders and guided her over to the entrance. Sabrina peeked inside and whistled. He took a certain amount of pride in that whistle—he had been so busy moving and sorting stuff all morning that he had developed a kind of tunnel vision. Now Sabrina's appreciation of his effort made it all worthwhile and helped him see all he'd accomplished.

"Think it'd make a good workshop?" he asked her.

"Workshop? For what?" she inquired.

"For you." He pulled her in against his side, knocking hips as he casually raised his coffee to his lips. "Surprise," he added.

Sabrina threw her arms around his neck unexpectedly, and Trevor nearly dropped his coffee. "Careful!" he laughed. As Sabrina hugged him fiercely, he thought he could feel a wet patch starting to form in his shirt. She drew away quickly and wiped her eyes.

"Sorry. It's just that...wow." She laughed to try to make light of her emotional response to his gesture. "I can't believe you're finally embracing this whole upcycling thing."

"I wouldn't call it exactly 'embracing' it," Trevor said. "But I figured if you're going to be sticking around here for a while, I might as well give you your own space to work out of. It will cut back on the junk piling up on the lawn, anyway."

"Oh, I plan on sticking around as long as you'll have me, Mr. Wild," she agreed. She rested her chin on his chest and gazed up at him. "No more coordinating new glamping programs and cutting out as soon as they're off the ground. My nomad days are far behind me. I intend to make sure *this* program in particular grows and thrives. And..."

Sabrina ducked her head away a little and blushed as she summoned the words. Trevor waited for her, ever patient, even as his heart hitched in anticipation.

"And I intend to make Wildhorse my home. If you'll agree to have me."

"No compromise needed on that front," he replied. When she glanced up curiously at his gruff tone, Trevor ensnared her in a surprise kiss. He felt her muffled sigh of contentment as she relaxed in his one-armed embrace. His neglected cup of coffee was probably growing cold by the second, but there was nothing he would rather taste on a Saturday morning than the woman he loved.

"Speaking of surprises..." Sabrina pulled away and headed back to the truck. "I picked something up for you in town."

Trevor watched her climb up onto the bed of the truck. He took a long sip from his mug. He hadn't had enough coffee yet to feel real apprehension at what she was about to show him. When he saw her struggling with something heavy, he quickly set his mug aside and jogged over to help. He had just hauled himself up after her when he saw what she was attempting to lift on her own. He froze in astonishment.

"You..." He couldn't find the words.

Sabrina straightened triumphantly and tucked a loose lock of blonde hair behind one ear. "Didn't think you'd like my surprise, did you?" she said with a laugh.

She stood over nothing other than his father's saddle—the one he had pawned and given up for lost weeks ago. The leather was freshly polished, and there wasn't a cinch or stirrup out of place. It looked better than he remembered.

"How did you...?" He trailed off in disbelief.

"I haven't only been going to the flea market every weekend to spend money," she explained. "I've been selling a lot of the stuff I've upcycled. I managed to sweet-talk the guy at the pawn shop to hold on to your dad's saddle until I could come up with the money." She waggled her eyebrows. "Surprised?

Trevor didn't know what to say. He didn't think there were words in the English language to convey how touched he was by her gesture. When was the last time he had asked anything of anyone? When was the last time anyone had gone out of their way to do a thing like this for him?

Sabrina bent and managed to lift the saddle into her arms all on her own. She grinned as she presented it to him. "What do you think? Want to take a break and go for a ride with me?" she asked.

He hadn't budgeted time for a ride in his weekend schedule. But Trevor knew his commitment to routine had transformed into a commitment to something—or someone—else. *Routine,* it turned out, wasn't any damn fun without someone around to challenge him to break out of it.

Trevor pulled the saddle out of her hands and grinned. "You're on."

END OF BREAKING THE COWBOY'S RULES

WILDHORSE RANCH BROTHERS

BOOK ONE

PLUS: Do you love billionaire playboys, cowgirls and naughty rides? Keep reading for an exclusive excerpt from Leslie North's bestselling novel, **Secret Billionaire's Stubborn Cowgirl,** Book One of The Secret Billionaires Series.

Thank You!

Thank you so much for purchasing and reading my book. It's hard for me to put into words how much I appreciate my readers. If you enjoyed this book, please remember to leave a review. I want to keep you guys happy! I love hearing from you :)

For all books by Leslie North visit:

Her Website: LeslieNorthBooks.com

Facebook: www.facebook.com/leslienorthbooks

Get SIX full-length, highly-rated Leslie North Novellas FREE! Over 548 pages of best-selling romance with a combined 634 FIVE STAR REVIEWS!

Sign-up to her mailing list and get your FREE books:

Leslienorthbooks.com/sign-up-for-free-books

Sneak Peek

SECRET BILLIONAIRE'S STUBBORN COWGIRL

Blurb

Zach Collins needed a break from the stress of his billion-dollar business and the stream of women eager to get their hands on his money. But when he set his sights on a simple country farm, he wasn't prepared to be working side by side with a firecracker like Lucy Ennis. She's stubborn, spirited and undeniably sexy, but as time goes by Zach can tell that her smiling eyes are hiding something. And while he's not willing to share his own secret, he's determined to unravel hers.

Lucy Ennis works hard to make ends meet. With a mountain of gambling debt left by her dead father and her mother in a nursing home she doesn't need any more trouble. So when she loses her job, she jumps at the chance to work at a farm being leased by a handsome stranger. With a Stetson hat atop bright blue eyes and chiseled abs, the man certainly comes in a sexy package, but he's also arrogant, inflexible, and doesn't seem to know much about farming. Despite her own problems piling up, Lucy can't help being drawn to the mystery man.

But as the intensity of their attraction grows, any chance at real happiness seems impossible when Zach continues to hide the truth and Lucy's shady past poses a very real threat.

Get your copy of the Secret Billionaire's Stubborn Cowgirl from www.LeslieNorthBooks.com

Excerpt

Lucy led him out to the old pond on Charlie's farm. It sat back from the road not far from the horse pasture. They'd kept their halters on the horses, so they tied them to a tree and Zach began pulling out the food.

Lucy sat down on the grass. "Oh, man! Charlie outdid herself this time."

It seemed like Zach just kept pulling food from his saddle bags. Fried chicken, biscuits, cheese and crackers, strawberries, even a bottle of wine and paper cups. He cracked open the wine—a twist-top, thank you, Charlie—and poured. "An excellent vintage, I see."

"Hey, don't knock the convenience." She leaned back on her elbows, sucking a strawberry into her mouth. The sweetness exploded and she closed her eyes and hummed. She looked up again to see Zach staring at her so intently that she had a hard time breathing. When his eyes dipped to her chest, she wondered if he could see the outline of her bra and breasts. His eyes darkened.

She caught a breath.

She didn't want this—but she did. She knew he was trouble—he wasn't the kind of guy she wanted. But he was what she needed right now.

He leaned over her, his mouth hovering close. All she had to do was push him away. All she had to do was crack a joke about employee harassment. All she had to do... god, he had beautiful eyes, the blue framed by thick, dark lashes.

He turned his head and kissed the crook of her neck. The warmth of his mouth undid the last of her good intentions. "Zach." His name slipped out on a whisper.

He pulled back. "Ask me."

She stared at him. "Ask you what?"

"Ask me to kiss you."

She shook her head. "Not a good idea."

"It's not a bad one. One kiss—what's the harm in one kiss?"

"Oh, I can think of a lot of harm."

He leaned closer. "Ask me anyway."

His eyes were her undoing. They teased her, light danced, tempted, promised, and she asked him by wrapping her hand around the back of his neck and pulling his mouth to hers.

She opened her mouth to him, to that kiss, to the need for him, raw, pure and simple. He pushed her down to the ground and she spread her legs so he could settle himself. She hadn't been with anyone like this since high school. She could feel his hands searching for a way under her shirt, a way to get to skin. She knocked off his Stetson and tangled her fingers in his hair.

A horse whinny pulled her back to reality—to what she was doing.

He pulled back and she sat up, pushing at her hair—he'd pulled it out of the pony tail. "That was some bottle of wine." She tried for a smile, but the joke fell flat.

"Lucy—"

She held up a hand. "One kiss. That's what you asked for—what I asked for. Best we leave it there."

"But—"

Pushing up to her feet, she stared down at him. "I can't quit. You don't want to fire me—not for that. So let's be smart about this." Bending down, she started to pack up the food. "Now we should head back, shouldn't we, boss? We've got clouds coming in and rain with 'em."

He shoved a hand into his hair and grabbed for his Stetson. "Don't think that leaves either of us satisfied."

Lucy pressed her lips tighter.

It didn't take long to pack the saddle bags, untie the horses and ride back. The wind picked up and the horses jogged, eager to get back to their pasture. At the trailer, Lucy focused on brushing down the mare, not on watching Zach—and not remembering that kiss. So what if he left her dizzy. So what if she'd been wet in five seconds. So what if she wanted to go back and grab him and kiss him again.

That was the trouble with guys like him—they spun your world around and then if you were fool enough to hook up with them they just kept on spinning you. Her daddy had been a man like that. Well, no thank you, sir. She wanted a hard-working man. She wanted a regular guy.

Zach headed into the trailer to put away his saddle.

That was when Lucy heard a sharp jingle and a bark. Fear ran up her back.

Get your copy of the Secret Billionaire's Stubborn Cowgirl from www.LeslieNorthBooks.com

Made in the USA
Lexington, KY
17 May 2017